XEROS

ZAK ZYZ

Cover and Interior Design by Zak Zyz - zakzyz.com
Black Falcon - Ceslav Sukstul - ceslavsukstul.com
Our Sun - Andrew James McCarthy - @cosmic_background
Arouet de Voltaire - Jean Antoine Houdon
Vrouw - Jan Luyken
Edited by Tim Marquitz - tmarquitz.com
Proofreading by Robert Butler
Mandarin proofreading by Holden Lee

By order of the Hezo Collective Prosperity Sphere:
Poems are rendered hengpai

SPECIAL THANKS TO THE SQUADRON!

ZYZ novels are edited in collaboration with a live internet audience. XEROS is far better thanks to their tireless contributions. Viewers receive one point per accepted edit.

EDIT ACE: LOJIK - 122
"I warn you to kill those you have defeated" CIL V 5933

SPATHI-WA - 109
ERA - 28
NEGI - 15
STRATUM - 13
MANTAS - 6
EMC^2 - 4
CHOOSEKNOWLEDGE - 3
ROGUE - 3
DIOXIDE - 3

Those who can make you believe absurdities
can make you commit atrocities

VOLTAIRE

The Dicta Boelcke

1. Try to secure advantages before attacking. If possible, keep the sun behind you.

2. Always carry through an attack when you have started it.

3. Fire only at close range and only when your opponent is properly in your sights.

4. Always keep your eye on your opponent, and never let yourself be deceived by ruses.

5. In any form of attack it is essential to assail your opponent from behind.

6. If your opponent dives on you, do not try to evade his onslaught but fly to meet it.

7. When over the enemy's lines never forget your own line of retreat.

8. Attack on principle in groups of four or six. When the fight breaks up into a series of single combats, take care that several do not go for one opponent.

0

Five minutes of space separated me from the interceptor squadron. My life flashed before my eyes, but I blinked it away. I didn't want to watch the re-run. Instead, I gazed at the growing silver ring where death waited, captivated by the idea this might be the final stroke.

If I died, the Hezo Collective Prosperity Sphere was finished. Tai Di would never permit this sort of idiocy again. Against the oppressive acceleration, the corners of my mouth twisted into a grin. It was perfect. My place in history would be secured.

I was the last dogfighter.

The first dogfight took place in 1913, during the Mexican Revolution. The planes were Curtiss and Christofferson Pushers, only slightly advanced from the Wright *Flyer 1* which first took wing at Kitty Hawk ten years before. Two airborne idiots took pot shots at each other with revolvers; both missed.

A year later, the first dogfighting 'victory' was claimed during the first week of World War I. A Russian pilot named Pyotr Nesterov rammed his Morane Parasol into a hapless Austrian Albatros, killing both men.

The tragi-comedy had escalated ever since. The bloody space battles at the Eye of Dagon and Da Jiao are barely skirmishes compared to the vast wars of our forefathers. Greatest of them was Blazar, the final confrontation between the sundered UNESECA navies.

Two implacable armadas clashed, furious as colliding galaxies. For eleven apocalyptic months, the two sides tore themselves apart until the very fabric of spacetime frayed. Five million ships thrown into the fire as fast as either side could build them.

Arietis Alpha and Beta are gone now, swallowed by a ceaseless interstellar storm. Nothing that flies in ever returns. Astronomers created a new designation for Ares-type nebulae: those born of war. They weren't fools, they knew there would be others.

If only I could have been there! If I could somehow slip past this squadron and complete the mission, I would be reborn as a spirit of war. I'd spend eternity drifting across the greatest battlefields of all time, drinking in the suffering of the ages. I could go questing into pre-history, seeking the root of all evil. A million years ago, some dark-eyed *xiong*, hefting a sharpened stone in his simian hand.

Of all the forbidden subjects, history was my favorite. I wanted to know it all, everything the Hezo had erased. Most of all, I wanted to see the first of my kind, the pilots. Those madmen who took to the skies and fought a world war in the days where we had just one world to lose. The Great War!

The lessons we learned in those first, fumbling dogfights are still being recited centuries later. Every combat pilot carries their legacy, pieces of shrapnel lodged too deep to ever work their way out.

I was a fitting end to the saga. A fool, tilting at a star. The utter quixotry! I barked a mad laugh into the compression fluid, for me alone.

My trenchant abandon was short-lived. The sun loomed ever larger in my canopy. Interceptors glittered in wait, positioned around the ring like shark teeth.

Desperation tightened in my throat. There must be some way to survive! Surely there was some angle I had missed, some tactic I hadn't considered. I couldn't slow down enough to activate my stealth field, I would burn up. The destroyer at my back was closing in.

I closed my eyes, praying for a sign from God, Tai Di, anyone. No one answered. I felt hollow. Old memories kept springing up, trying to break through my drug-fueled fixation. The silver ring of death became the iris of a cold gray eye.

Tsuros! That great human furnace, blazing with animus the moment he saw me. Somehow, he knew all along I was the one. The other inmates were only props, cast aside the instant their use was through. I was his tool, a lance hurled at the eye of God. The idea left me twisting with want. I wanted to be used. I wanted to be expended.

Three minutes to impact, three minutes to certain death. I shut my eyes and let my mind run wild.

My very first day in the Xeros program, Sergeant Tsuros hit me with an ancient piece of air combat doctrine called the *Dicta Boelcke*. I mean that literally. He crumpled up the sheet of paper and bounced it off my forehead. Like a fool, I darted a hand out and caught it before it hit the ground.

It was our first day on the station. None of us knew any better, no one had even been culled yet. A few dopes even laughed. Not me. From the first moment, I knew Tsuros was the dangerous one, the viper among the garters. His expression grew dark. A storm was coming.

The violence was swift and thorough. I remember lying on the deck, bleeding with the other recruits. There must have been cries of pain all around me, but all I could hear was boots. Tsuros stomped over and hoisted me up by my collar. He dangled me from one hand without effort, as if we were in zero-G. The wad of paper was still clutched in my hand.

"Nice catch, Traitor. Memorize those by 0400 tomorrow. Fuck up and it's double."

He discarded me like a piece of trash. I remember wondering when we'd be taken for medical treatment. *Hah!*

When I could move again, I tried to memorize the sheet, but the numbers swam on the page. Trying to read felt like putting weight on a broken ankle. I had a serious concussion. But I had no choice but to try anyway. Another beating would kill me. All night long, I mouthed the words while the other inmates twisted and groaned in their bunks.

The handwritten page was a set of eight rules, entitled *Dicta Boelcke*. Since the era of biplanes, combat pilots have studied them. When 0400 arrived, I could barely stand up. I recited the eight dicta word for word. Tsuros glared at me, making a *tchip* of annoyance with the side of his mouth.

He'd been hoping I would fuck up, and I had disappointed him. My reward was a slap across the mouth, hard enough to turn my head. It confused me, not because I expected anything else, but because I found I was disappointed, too.

I had a lot to learn about myself. The moment burned into me, along with the dicta. I can never forget.

I blinked back to the controls. Sixty seconds to intercept. I had no plan. I realized I was breaking all eight dicta. I was outnumbered and outgunned, flying straight into the sun. My squadron was gone, there was no line of retreat. Sixty seconds to contact. There was only one question left: How did I want to die?

时难年荒世业空
弟兄羁旅各西东
田园寥落干戈后
骨肉流离道路中
弔影分为千里雁
辞根散作九秋蓬
共看明月应垂泪
一夜乡心五处同

1
TRAITOR

"What is your crime?" Sergeant Tsuros demanded.

"I betrayed mankind. I collaborated with the enemy."

"What is your name?"

"Traitor."

The drill sergeant turned his back on me. One by one, the other inmates in the training flight followed suit. They did this every self-critique, and it always hurt in a deep way no physical punishment could. I have to hand it to Tsuros, he was a master. Since that first painful day, I had hung on his every word. I believed the sermons. I hated myself for betraying the human race, and I was prepared to die to redeem myself.

The shine wore off. I can remember the exact moment it happened. It was a few days after a struggle session. Sergeant Tsuros screamed in my face, howling at me about a pimple-sized divot of rust he'd discovered on a latrine pipe.

It wasn't my job to clean this particular latrine. If it were, every millimeter would have been spotless. I was always squared away. The pipe shouldn't have rusted, either. It was supposed to be stainless steel. But as the war dragged on, it was harder and harder to find real parts.

Not long ago, High Command had outlawed onsite fabricators across the entire Hezo Collective Prosperity Sphere. They were trying to re-establish the old logistical chains, to spin up ancient factories and revert to the old ways. It wasn't going well at all. Too much had been forgotten.

The trickle of spare parts we received were misshapen and rife with impurities. After a lifetime of molecularly immaculate environs, the shoddy wartime materials felt like a chipped tooth. It must have been worse for the drills. Manifesting obsessive-compulsive behavior was their entire job.

I happened to be standing closest to Sergeant Tsuros when he discovered the rusty latrine pipe, so I took the fall. I knew better than to argue.

I stood at attention as Tsuros screamed into my ear. If I flinched, the next thing I would feel was his fist in my gut. If the punch dropped me, there would be a boot in the ribs to follow it up. That was how Tsuros operated. I'd only caught the follow-up boot once, and that was enough for me. It hurt to breathe for an entire week afterward.

Sergeant Tsuros circled as he berated me. It was unusual to get chewed-out for so long, especially for such a minor infraction. There was an inordinate tension in his voice.

If I were allowed to speak, I could have told Tsuros I felt the same way he did. I hated the incompetence. I hated to see things crumbling that should always be strong. I hated being a prisoner, sealed in this barracks. I hated the other inmates who were always screwing up and pulling me down with them. I hated myself.

Sergeant Tsuros came to a halt with his gray eyes searing me, the tip of his nose a millimeter from mine.

"We are in a war! A war for SURVIVAL! A war for our EXISTENCE! And you can't keep a toilet clean! A FUCKING TOILET!" A fleck of spittle struck me in the eye as Tsuros screamed in my face. I winced, turning slightly aside. *What an error!* I was certain he would clobber me for it.

But Tsuros didn't hit me. At least not right away. I blinked and struggled to regain my bearing. He looked at me a way no other drill ever had. It froze me in place. It was a look of concern. The man honestly hadn't meant to spit in my eye.

It was an accident.

In that indelible moment, I realized we were losing the war. The endless drills, the sermons, the self-critique sessions, it was all pointless. It didn't matter if the latrine was spotless or spewing raw sewage until the barracks were ankle deep. We were losing.

Tsuros knew. He hid it behind his endless scorn, the fixation on cleanliness, the obsession with order. But the mask had slipped. Now, I knew, and I could never forget.

To break the tension, Tsuros inhaled sharply through his nose and spat fully in my face. He followed up with a slap that whipped my head hard-starboard. I was so stunned I couldn't even feel it.

Finished with me, Tsuros moved down the line to the next prisoner. He howled about a strand of hair he'd found in the airlock liner. I struggled to stay on my feet.

How could we be losing?

I wasn't stupid. Even as a prisoner locked in the window-less barracks, I'd suspected the war was going poorly. Our squadron was housed at the very edge of the station's habitat disc, but I still felt it when a supply ship docked.

The UNESECA freighters were enormous, and their vibrations hummed through the entire station. That feeling always filled me with dread. For days after a docking, the drills became doubly sadistic. The ships always brought bad news.

When they swapped us to vat-grown rations, the drills told us it was a punishment for our last inspection. But I could smell it on their breath as they shouted in my face. They were eating the same swill as us. The supply lines had been cut.

The drills used to have radios, I'm sure of it. They used to chatter with each other incessantly. Coordinating training, calling in injuries, and speculating on what might be for lunch. When an inmate did something especially stupid, they would get on the horn and guffaw about it with the other drills.

That resonated in me. They were laughing at us in a private way, but they did it while we were standing right in front of them. Letting us know we didn't matter at all. I liked that.

One day, the radios were all gone. Two of the softer drills weren't seen again afterward. A few members of my training flight were pulled out and permanently reassigned as gofers. We were told it was a reward. But why had they rewarded the most useless lumps in the flight? Why did they pass over me?

It didn't make sense, but little did. Despite all the signs things were going poorly, until Tsuros spit in my eye, I truly believed we were winning the war. We had to! For three formations a day, the drills barked at us that victory was destiny. It was imperative I do my utmost for the cause.

The barracks had to be spick-and-span, our answers during self-critique had to be instantaneous and impeccable. We had to have perfect faith in the Hezo at all times. Doubters would be disposed of.

The constant drilling, the sleep deprivation, and the isolation had leeched the color out of everything. My memories of my life before I was captured were as thin and insubstantial as soap bubbles. I think I would have even forgotten my crime if the drills hadn't made it my name.

I believed with all my heart I deserved this, that the punishment was just. This was a war for the survival of the human race! Our sins would be redeemed. Victory was destiny! We simply had to do what we were told.

I could do what I was told. But I couldn't forget the look on Sergeant Tsuros' face. In the weeks that followed, I appreciated why he was so vicious. It wasn't just that we were stupid and incompetent, though we certainly were. Tsuros envied our ignorance. It was a terrible burden to know this was all a farce, that we were losing. I was filled with nostalgia for the faith I could never recapture.

I knew if Tsuros even suspected I had figured him out, he would have me executed. I had to feign the zeal I no longer felt. I worked harder than the others and volunteered for all the worst duties.

Whenever a drill singled me out, I was certain my time had come. It was exhausting. Finally, something inside me broke. I wished the drills would just kill me and get it over with. I started to coast and expected to be dead within a week.

But every time I thought I was done for, some other inmate screwed up worse. They broke the rules, they missed their milestones, they said stupid things during self-critique. We all had to line up outside the airlock to watch their executions. Through the thick porthole window, I watched their mute pleas. I scrutinized their weeping faces for any sign they'd figured it out. I never found it. They hadn't realized we were losing, they were just weak.

I was a coward and a fraud. I was a traitor. But I was never weak. One by one, the others were given to the void. I had been imprisoned in the rings of Keilu with forty-five other inmates. Forty of us survived the long journey in the wretched prison barge. I was the last passenger still alive. I kept waiting for my turn, but it never came.

For three beautiful months, I was left alone. I haunted the empty barracks, ecstatic there was no one left who could get me in trouble. I ate double rations alone in a cafeteria meant to operate constantly, seating a thousand people per shift. The drills still pretended to find mistakes to berate me for, but their hearts weren't in it. The beatings stopped. There was no point without an audience.

It was better than freedom, if only because I couldn't remember what freedom was like. Even in my dreams, I was still trapped in the unchanging gray barracks.

It couldn't last. Unbeknownst to me, there were other training flights being winnowed down in the other sectors of the station. Mine had been the fastest to eliminate its undesirables, so my barracks became the staging area for the next flight.

One by one, other survivors arrived, and my lovely solitude ebbed away. The drills formed us into a squadron, and the second phase began.

重帏深下莫愁堂，卧后清宵细细长。

神女生涯原是梦，小姑居处本无郎。

风波不信菱枝弱，月露谁教桂叶香。

直道相思了无益，未妨惆怅是清狂。

2
MURDERESS

"What is your crime?"

"I killed the future."

"What is your name?"

"Murderess."

"You are empty," Sergeant Tsuros would say, concluding the ritual. Then he'd punch Murderess in the stomach, hard enough to drive the air from her lungs. I must have watched her sobbing for breath on the floor a dozen times.

I was always a little too interested, and the others could tell. Everyone was required to watch, but only I wanted to. I knew it repulsed the others, but I didn't care. There were so few things in this place I truly enjoyed and seeing that cunt get belted was always the highlight of my month.

Murderess was beyond stubborn. When the Hezo ordered her to keep her baby, she declined. Openly! All she had to do was feign complications like everyone else. But she just had to take a stand.

I don't know who hated her worse, the inmates or the drills. The drills hated her for her crime. The squadron hated her for getting us in trouble. We soaked up so much collective punishment for that woman and her opposition-defiant disorder. She was one of those people who had to test every boundary, but she was also a slow learner and never shut up.

It was a truly unfortunate combination for everyone. I got the feeling all the drills wanted to execute her, but they'd been overruled. When the drills are unhappy, it means the rest of us are miserable. The week Murderess joined the squadron, I went to bed every night expecting to find her strangled in the morning. No one did it. I think we were all hoping someone else would.

In her defense, things were rigged against Murderess from the start. She was a late arrival, replacing an inmate who died from an *accident*. The squad was undergoing ship acclimation, which was an especially awful time.

We were all recovering from brain surgery, irritable and prone to bouts of senseless rage. The surgeons fitted us with pilot interfaces, three shiny black dots on either temple. Our vestibular systems were chopped up and re-arranged to allow us to survive high-G space combat. There was an awful price to pay, five days of crippling nausea and constant vertigo. Our suffering was hysterical to the drills. They laughed at us as we stumbled and clung to the walls for support, tipping us over for sport. Anyone who didn't get up right away caught a boot. We learned to walk again in a hurry.

During the acclimation process, the drills sealed us inside our ships to check for adverse reactions. Not from us, of course. If we got rashes or if our faces swelled up and couldn't breathe, that was just too bad. It was the ships the drills were worried about.

Being sealed inside the Yama was the most unpleasant thing I've ever experienced. It felt like I was stuck against the roof of a giant's mouth and he was trying to scrape me off with his tongue. The ships were built to keep us in homeostasis; comfort was irrelevant. Each was supposed to be molecularly keyed to its pilot. But like everything the Hezo did, there was a tendency to fail.

Murderess's predecessor was an inmate named Toucher, a slug-tongued outcast no one liked. I can remember his slobbery voice as he pleaded with the drills. He begged them not to make him get back into the ship. Of course, this only made the drills seal him inside for twice as long.

When the drills popped the Yama's hatch, they didn't pull Toucher out as much as pour him out. His ship had closed around him like a fist and crushed him into a paste. We all saw it. Worse, we all smelled it. Nobody slept that night, but there was nothing to do but pray it didn't happen to us.

The drills were on edge, too. They must have caught hell for crushing that poor fool. They had to find a replacement for him.

Murderess was one of the gofer washouts. She had a background in logistics, so they assigned her to assist the quartermaster. It must have been a rude awakening, thinking she'd miraculously survived only to be sucked back into the nightmare.

They had to build a new ship for her, so she had nothing to do while we acclimated. It wasn't exactly endearing to see her watching from the sidelines as we all suffered.

I tried to empathize, to be nice to her. I was the only one. Many times, I offered her a bit of advice or a shoulder to cry on. She declined. I was attracted to her, and she wasn't attracted to me.

The story of my life.

绛帻鸣人送晓筹
尚衣方进翠云裘
九天阊阖开宫殿
万国衣冠拜冕旒
日色才临仙掌动
香烟欲傍衮龙浮
朝罢须裁五色诏
佩声归向风池头

3
PIRATE

"What is your crime?"

"I deserted my post. I stole from the Collective Prosperity Sphere. I attacked vital shipments and jeopardized the war effort. I plundered and reaved."

"What is your name?

"Pirate."

"You are a parasite. Take from him as he took from all of us."

Each of us had to line up in front of Pirate and take a piece out of him. We were required to grab a tangle of his thick black hair and rip it out by the roots. Once, Glutton didn't tug hard enough.

I remember the panic in his face, the way he frantically tugged again, hoping the drill hadn't noticed. Of course, they did. The drill stormed over, hissing curses.

"THIS IS HOW YOU DO IT!" the drill barked, grabbing a fistful of Glutton's fine blond hair. He yanked so hard Glutton's scalp seeped blood for the rest of the day. Nobody screwed up the ritual after that. Pirate was a hirsute man, but after a few struggle sessions, it was hard to find a handful of hair anywhere on his body. He looked like a badly plucked chicken.

I hated the other members of the squadron from the start. First, I hated them for robbing me of my isolation. Soon, I hated them for their incompetence, all the punishments I suffered on their behalf. Some idiot lost two sewing needles, and we had to rip the entire barracks apart looking for them, three times in a row.

When they didn't turn up, the squadron was given twenty-four hours of no rations as punishment. I seethed about it, but what could I do? Nothing but hate, hate, hate, and keep my mouth shut. I fantasized about killing them, but I wasn't stupid enough to try.

I was the youngest and the smallest by far. Even Murderess was ten centimeters taller than me, and I hated her for that, too. I hated them all.

Except Pirate. The others hated him so much. I liked him just to spite them. When the drills weren't around, Pirate swelled up with a bottomless confidence. No amount of violent depilation could squelch his swagger.

Every day, Pirate would spin a new yarn as we scrubbed and mopped the barracks until it was as spotless as a surgical ward. He told his tales with a rolling, self-important cadence as if he were reciting the *Odyssey*. Impossible stories about looting freighters, breaking comrades out of prisons, out-running pursuers, and bedding a seemingly endless stream of wide-eyed damsels.

You could roll your eyes, you could call him a liar, you could walk away from him, it didn't matter. The man was in love with the sound of his own voice. He would keep talking, following you around, and there was nowhere to hide in the barracks. I have never met a sober man so utterly impervious to criticism.

The other inmates tried to tune Pirate out, but I liked to wind him up with little nods to keep him going. I started doing it to infuriate the others, but, in time, I realized I liked listening to him. There were always a few maddening kernels of indigestible truth lodged in his bullshit.

Pirate claimed he was the result of a forbidden liaison between two high-ranking Polomen. He fit the mold; wide-set eyes, an aquiline beak of a nose, insufferable vanity. His was an old story. A child of privilege begins life with seemingly limitless potential and amounts to nothing at all.

"I was destined to be a great sculptor!" Pirate proclaimed as the others rolled their eyes and distanced themselves. He shouldered his mop like a rifle. "The greatest! Marvelous marble, beautiful bronze, sublime steel, myriad masterpieces in every media. It was my dream since I was a child!

"I studied under the great L'orze Del Dico! I was her most exemplary pupil, her most passionate lover. Alas, I shone too bright! My application to the Academy of Revolutionary Arts was declined! The cowards knew I would eclipse them! In their pettiness, they engineered to have me drafted. Imagine that, the great Pirate, conscripted as a lowly mechanic!"

Pirate made grandiose gestures at Addict. Addict wheezed and bent to scour a drain grating that was already spotless.

Corrupt watched from across the barracks with an old toothbrush in his hand. He had a smile that always meant trouble.

"Surely there was a greater need for mechanics than sculptors, brother. Are you saying the Hezo was wrong to draft you?" Corrupt angled. His blue eyes gleamed with ill-intent. Corrupt had been cleaning the dust from the aluminum vanes of the radiator. He always slurped up the easiest tasks.

Pirate's eyes were green, edged with gold. They lit up at the unexpected acknowledgement of his existence. He sauntered over to the radiator with his mop. I smiled as Corrupt winced. The fool had only been fishing for something to snitch about, now Pirate had latched onto him instead of Addict.

"No, comrade! Nothing could be farther from the truth! It was wise, very wise of the Hezo! I became the greatest mechanic in the entire Prosperity Sphere. I had the great honor of being sent to the Tau Ceti Front. I served honorably on the ORB of Ahklys."

Pirate puffed up his chest, and the barracks grew deathly silent.

"What's an ORB?" I asked, though I already knew what it stood for. I knew just about everything a civilian was allowed to know about spacecraft, and plenty they weren't. I just wanted to steer the conversation away from the dangerous course Pirate had charted.

"An Orbital Repair Bay. It was enormous! A hundred times bigger than this dismal disk. We had capital ships in those days. They were glorious! I can remember watching the fleet launch into the ruby dust. Like a grand caravan, vanishing into a sirocco!"

"I never heard of any Tau Ceti Front," Glutton protested, and Addict chittered in agreement. I don't think they were teasing Pirate or acting out of malice. Those two were just clueless about anything you couldn't shoot, snort, or eat.

"There was no Tau Ceti Front," Corrupt pronounced. Here was the malice. Corrupt and Murderess shared a poisonous glance. Liar had only been half-listening as he scrubbed on the other side of the barracks. When he realized what we were talking about, he abandoned his brush and shrank away into the latrine. Corrupt used to be a governor, Murderess was in logistics, and Liar had been what passed for a journalist in the Hezo. They all knew.

A sound of protest died in Pirate's throat. Corrupt smiled a serrated grin. Pirate looked toward Murderess for help, but she gave him nothing. Finally, Pirate turned to me, with a childish, pleading expression.

"There was no Tau Ceti Front. You must be thinking of another," I said, more softly than Corrupt had. I looked from face to face, trying to tell if the others knew how serious this was. If the drills caught wind of this conversation, we were all going to die.

Pirate's face fell, no one on his side. But then, I winked at him. It wasn't subtle, and the others all stared at me. I glared back, daring them to snitch. I would gladly drag them all down to Hell with me.

Pirate returned a tight-lipped nod of understanding. He went back to swabbing the floor with sullen swipes of the mop. There was a strained silence in the barracks for the rest of the morning.

Officially, there was never a Tau Ceti Front. There was never even a Tau Ceti, the official Hezo star maps omit it, daring anyone to disagree. But I've seen files. I've seen footage.

Tau Ceti was a slaughter.

The next day, Pirate was himself again. To punish us for Murderess existing, the drills had ordered us to muck out a hydraulic lift flooded with spoiled bio-oil. It was like swimming in a cesspool.

Most of us wore masks against the stench, but Pirate's mask had ridden down to his neck. The smell didn't bother him. He was engrossed in telling us a story.

"...the Hezo ace, Redbeak. The nose of his ship was painted crimson, as if wet with blood. He tracked me across five systems before he caught me. I was low on gas, trying to refuel at Gliese-Songhua. What a beauty! She was a helium Niflheim of burning ice, where thousand-kilometer crystal spires wept away into the void."

Corrupt made a gagging noise. It was unclear whether he'd been disgusted by the rotting oil or Pirate's histrionics. I tried to scowl at him to shut up, but the impact was muted by my mask.

"Gliese-Songhua has two tails, like a comet. One gas and one dust. I was in the gas trail, drinking greedily, unaware Redbeak lay in ambush! He waited until my tanks were deployed and I was vulnerable, the coward! I was caught by surprise, but I had a trick up my sleeve, oh, yes! I jettisoned a tank! His first salvo missed by millimeters! My ship was intact, but I was in a desperate plight. I was down to the last dregs of oxygen, caught in a dogfight with a Hezo ace!"

Corrupt yawned theatrically. Beneath the muck, I checked him with the blade of my shovel, making satisfying contact with his shinbone.

"Sorry!" I faux-pologized.

Corrupt hissed at me, and I tightened my grip on the shovel. For a few seconds, I thought the two of us might go at it. But any fight here would end with both of us coated in rancid oil. I was willing, Corrupt wasn't. Pirate continued on, oblivious.

"For what felt like hours, we darted through the trails of ice and fog, seeking one another. Pass after pass, guns blazing, like knights tilting through the mist. At last, my head pounded, there was a clawing in my chest, and I knew it would be my final chance. I took that last turn at full throttle. My vision went gray, and I thought I'd died from acceleration alone."

"When my sight returned, there was Redbeak, dead in my sights! He was executing the same maneuver, but he was a split-second less daring than I. It was the death of him! The bloody-nosed hunter fell into the gravity well in a thousand pieces, and I was triumphant!"

Pirate raised a fist, his eyes blazing. I'd stopped bailing muck to listen to him.

"My victory was nearly pyrrhic. I barely had the strength to activate the reclaimer. Then there was a terrible hour where I lay motionless at the controls, trying to conserve every molecule of oxygen. I am certain I was less than ten breaths away from suffocating when the reactor caught up with me. Bless the man who invented triple-alpha conversion!"

"Her name was Antoinette Bakers-Lin," Murderess sniped. From the tilt of her eyebrows, there was a fierce scowl beneath her mask.

"No, it was a man. Fred Hoyle," Liar argued, never missing a chance to antagonize Murderess. But they were both wrong, and they were in my territory now: ships. I saw a rare chance to pile on both of them at once, and I leapt on it.

"Hoyle discovered the process, the 7.656 MeV carbon-12 resonance. He used to run around claiming it meant there had to be a *superintelligence* responsible. You know how that turned out. Bakers-Lin created the first real proof of concept for a converter, but her version was inefficient, and no one adopted it. Back then, we were building generation ships and mass wasn't as much of an issue. It was only when the UNESECA came out with nimbus-folding reactors someone remembered her idea and refined it. Triple-alpha conversion was a big factor in the spread of the UNESECA empire. They could field much smaller ships than their rivals. We don't know who invented the modern design, but it has little in common with the Bakers-Lin prototype."

I rattled off my little history lesson without pausing to consider the wisdom of doing so. I was just annoyed at Murderess and Liar for interrupting Pirate's story. Now, the others stared at me, and I realized I'd slipped up.

"How do you know all that, kid?" Murderess asked, eyes narrowed.

I knew this conversation would make its way into a drill's ear. I needed to attempt an evasive maneuver of my own.

"That's basic history, ma'am. You should have learned it in primary school, but you never pay attention. That's why your flight scores are like this," I motioned to the knee-deep filth we waded in.

Her face grew molten. I had her. In reality, I had never gone to school at all. Everything I knew, I had learned sifting through the illegal nets on Keilu.

Murderess fumed at me for hours, and I pointedly ignored her. The others kept growling at her to shut up. If the drills showed up, we would all suffer. They were all mad at me, too, for setting her off.

I didn't care. My gambit worked. The jibe made Murderess so angry, she forgot all about what I'd said before.

It was a miserable morning. A harpy bitching in my ears, the whole squadron mad at me, and a seemingly endless supply of vile swill underfoot. I kept shoveling, daydreaming about dogfighting in the twin tails of Gliese-Songhua.

If only I could be Pirate for a day, to finally separate truth from fiction! But it was more than that. I wished I had his confidence, his seeming invulnerability. I wanted all the things about him that were so much more than me.

I thought about it with the same lurid hunger as when I imagined taking a shower in Murderess' body. Ever since I was a boy, that'd been my favorite mind-game, imagining myself as others to pass the time. Anyone else would be an improvement.

功盖三分国
名成八阵图
江流石不转
遗恨失吞吴

4
CORRUPT

"What is your crime?"

"I robbed from those in my care. I stole from the mouths of children."

"What is your name?"

"Corrupt."

"You are a worm, lower than dirt! Get down where you belong, scum."

Tsuros would gut-punch Corrupt, dropping him like an empty sack. After that, the whole squadron had to march on him, grinding him into the deck. It was a delicate balance; if we stomped too hard, he'd be useless and we'd have to work harder to pick up his slack. If a drill caught us stepping too gingerly, we'd share his fate.

I never had that problem. If no one else was there, I would have jumped up and down on his spine like a trampoline until he was dead or paralyzed. Obviously, I've spent some time thinking about it.

Corrupt was a bureaucrat from Niejingdiyu, who was found guilty of planetary-scale embezzlement. His crimes nearly defied belief, theft so flagrant even the Hezo couldn't stomach it. That's like being so shitty flies won't land on you. It made me smile, knowing I was scrubbing toilets shoulder to shoulder with a man who used to be the Governor of Ushan's largest moon.

Corrupt was in his mid-fifties. He was blue-eyed and serpent-tongued, standing two meters tall with a swoop of thinning blond hair and a perpetual smirk. Three qualities had propelled him through the Hezo: he was good-looking, his family was well-connected, and he would tell anyone anything he thought they wanted to hear.

Corrupt was one of those tiresome prisoners who never quite realized there had been no mistake. Prison was exactly where he belonged, forever. He couldn't accept this, couldn't process there was no talking his way out of this predicament. A lamprey would have blushed at the way he sucked up to the drills. He was forever in earshot, ready to tattle at the slightest infraction. When the going was smooth, he liked to pretend he was our leader. When things went sideways, he was the first to shift blame.

I despised him.

Corrupt tried me one morning when I'd drawn airlock cleaning duty. It was a meticulous task. Tsuros liked to whip out the white gloves, whistling *Boléro* as he went over every nanometer of the airlock interior. If he found the slightest speck, the whistling would stop, but the inspection would go on. The screwup inmate would stand at attention in silence, awaiting the inevitable beating. A blown airlock inspection meant a trip to the infirmary, every time.

The other inmates were usually relieved when I drew lock duty; I never failed. But Corrupt had a funny look that morning. As I was headed to the lock, he stepped into my path and dressed me down for not cleaning the underside of the slop sink. The drills never even checked the slop sink.

I thought he must be joking. The squadron never got in trouble because of me, not once. But he meant it. This upright parasite, who once embezzled the funding meant to feed *an entire moon*, somehow dared to chide me. I tried to walk away, but Corrupt followed me and kept needling.

He got under my skin. I wheeled around on him, holding the lock-knocker in my hand. The lead-cored mallet was part of of the airlock cleaning kit. It took a few good whacks to get the ancient safety latch to release. I figured a couple taps would be enough to disengage Corrupt's jaw. The drills would execute me, but what did it matter? We were condemned.

I grinned and stepped closer.

The look in his eyes!

Corrupt went from tormentor to terrified in a spasm of glorious transilience. He held up his palms and shrank away, a timid smile like he'd only been joking. I glared at him until he left the room. One more word and I would have brained him.

After that, he wouldn't be alone with me. It was an unexpected bonus, until the other inmates started shying away too. Corrupt told them I'd gone rabid and flipped on him for no reason. I didn't bother to challenge him, no one would believe me. I had always been apart from the other inmates. Now I was isolated.

It took a few days for me to understand how I'd lost the exchange. I'd written Corrupt off as a complete imbecile and wondered how in Diyu anyone had ever let him be in charge of a moon. But Corrupt wasn't oblivious, he was *operating.* Everything he did had intent. He was a sapper, undermining the others to shore up his own shaky foundation. He would tug Pirate one way to wind him up and nudge Murderess another to make her unravel. Then he would tie the two threads together and wait for the imbroglio to erupt. He got off on it, maneuvering the rest of the squadron into these little passion plays where he was always the hero. Once I was on the outside of his little web, it was easy to see the strands.

Corrupt's favorite weapon was an innocuous-seeming comment that ate in like acid. He asked Murderess how she'd broken her nose. When she asked him what he was babbling about, he shrugged it off. Days later I caught her at the latrine mirror, squinting at her reflection as she turned her head side to side. *He had her.*

Soon he was acting as her confidant, telling her all the shitty things the other inmates said about her. There was no shortage of them. Liar had called her "that balding bitch!" when he found a bunch of her hair in the shower drain. It got a big laugh, we were all losing our hair from stress and the terrible diet. Corrupt omitted the self-deprecating context when he ratted and spun it as a dire insult.

Murderess confronted Liar and, of course, he lied, claiming he'd never said it. Addict contradicted him. Liar was caught and it was too late to explain he hadn't meant anything by it. They got in a terrible fight, screaming so loud the rest of us had to shut them up before they drew the drills.

During a flight exercise two days later, Murderess listed her ship dangerously close to Liar's. Liar kept banking, trying to get clear. Murderess wouldn't let up. She nearly chased him out of the bounds of the exercise.

If it had gone on for ten more seconds, the drills would have shot both of them down. Afterward, the whole squadron got two days of no rations as punishment.

I'd learned from the sewing needle incident and had stashed a tiny bit of food in the right-hand side of the latrine vent over the toilet. My emergency rations were foil packets of vatchup, the pungent, vat-grown ketchup we were issued once per week at chow. I sucked them down like a vampire in the dead of the night, rolling them into tight little spirals to extract every atom of fake tomato paste.

I hid the wrappers in the vent until I could find a way to dispose of them. The drills only felt arm-deep during inspection, so I pushed them out of reach with the short-handled mop.

The others weren't so prescient. Towards the end of the punishment, they were coming unglued, wobbly and frantic with hunger. Murderess and Liar got into it again, shouting and shoving. It was dangerous. If a drill came, one of them was getting airlocked. Maybe both.

Corrupt stepped in, playing the diplomat. He knew exactly how to defuse the bomb because he had built it.

"This has to stop! We all buried an entire flight to get here. All of us were *chosen*. Don't throw it away! Remember the mission and start thinking like a squadron. We have to succeed, the Hezo needs us! If we work hard and watch each other's backs, we will succeed. We can be heroes. Our names will ring out for thousands of years!"

I remember listening to his spiel and thinking it would fall flat, that no one could be that stupid.

Everyone bought it. They all treated Corrupt like a hero for breaking up the fight. He beamed for a week afterward. Like an arsonist-fireman, mugging for the camera with a singed kitten in his hands.

Though I was wise to his game, I didn't interfere. In prison, anything that breaks up the monotony is invaluable. I kept expecting the others to wise up and turn on Corrupt, but they never did. Were they that stupid, or were they willing participants in the charade? Either way, I had to laugh.

Watching Sergeant Tsuros, I had learned we were losing the war. Watching Corrupt, I learned why.

We're just too stupid to survive.

清秋幕府井梧寒
独宿江城蜡炬残
永夜角声悲自语
中天月色好谁看
风尘荏苒音书绝
关塞萧条行陆难
已忍伶俜十年事
强移栖息一枝安

5
SILHOUETTES

Why am I still alive?

With every execution I watched, the question became harder to answer. In my first training flight, I watched thirty-nine inmates get airlocked. All of them were better than me in every way the Hezo could want. They were older, stronger, and better educated. True believers, dripping with zeal. Into the vacuum they went, here in the barracks I remained.

I spent my nights peering at the ceiling in the faint crimson light wondering, *Why me?*

I was the youngest person on the station by a decade. The Hezo captured me when I was fifteen years old. I lost track of time after that, but I couldn't be much older than twenty. I was a baby. Murderess was forty-one, Corrupt was fifty-five.

Pirate was *old*. His body was that of a man in his mid-forties, but there was a Methuselaean cast to his eyes, a century-deep weariness at odds with his cheerful demeanor and incessant yammering. It was taboo to mention his age-lessness.

The Xian-Zwitterion Process had been outlawed in the Hezo for generations. Most who'd undergone it had defected to the Collaborators early in the war, or else they'd been executed. But there were still a few like Pirate floating around, jutting stones in the river of time.

Other than a knack for cleaning toilets perfectly, there's not much to me. I never did anything interesting with my life like the others. Washed-up child gambler, trolling the nets, part-time mechanic, then prison. I wasn't beautiful, nor ugly. I was short and skinny from the shit rations like everyone else. Just a big zero. Why did they keep me around?

I suppose I showed promise as a pilot, at least compared to the others. It wasn't a high bar. We only flew basic exercises, but Pirate and I were at the top of the pack. He edged me out now with experience, but my circuit times were climbing faster than his. I knew I would overtake him. The legacy of a misspent youth.

Before the nets were cut and the arcades were shuttered, I used to play a space-battle simulator called *MARTYR*. It was a blatant recruiting tool for the Hezo Navy. They set the consoles up in the poorest habs of Ring 5, which was by far the worst of Keilu's eight artificial rings.

It was free to play, and the graphics were incredible. You strapped in a special gyroscopic isolation pod that let you feel every shot. There were leaderboards and prizes, a tidy little bit of propaganda. The joke was, if you did too well in a game, you would open the hatch and find a recruiter waiting for you.

It wasn't a joke. When I was ten or eleven, I tried to run with the big dogs in a free-for-all deathmatch. There were a couple of tournament guys playing. I was doing well at first, but it didn't matter. We all got dumpstered by an arcade ace who went by the handle *OBS*.

By my second death, he was up fourteen kills with zero deaths. I couldn't land a shot on him. I tore off my harness and rage-ejected, screaming he was a cheater.

Then, I saw the three men standing outside of his pod.

I shut up in a hurry. On the overhead display, it flashed the final score, twenty-three to nil.

OBS was all smiles when he emerged, then he saw the Navy guys waiting for him. They did all the smiling after that, clapping the big winner on the back, congratulating him. They led him away, and it was clear he had no choice in the matter.

Twenty-three to nil.

I remember talking with the other players, calling OBS a try-hard idiot for stunting on us. What kind of moron would keep playing after they turned sixteen? But as I got older, I appreciated the trap they'd laid for us. The game was all we had. We were all deck-poor debt-slaves, scavenging for scraps in the lowest hab tier. Not even basic edu. None of us would ever climb out of this pit.

But, in the game, we could fly. When you were winning, you felt totally free, above everything and everyone. I understood why OBS couldn't stop playing. I promised myself I wouldn't let it happen to me. I would make enough to buy my freedom and retire from gambling. I would be free.

Look at me now. I stretched out my hands to the crimson emptiness of the barracks ceiling. *Free.* It was nobody's fault but my own.

"All right, simpletons! Time to play *Name That Plane!*"

The other inmates flinched, hunching their shoulders and shrinking into themselves. Silhouette training usually ended in vicious beatings. But not for me. In the classroom, we were only accountable for our own stupidity. I could finally watch the others reap their own ineptitude without suffering alongside them.

The display wall was cold and dead. Taking its place, a roll-down screen had been bolted to the ceiling with plumber's tape. My eyes lasered in on an orange fringe of rust accumulating on the new bolts.

I needed to remember to scour that off the next time we were ordered to clean the classroom.

Tsuros tugged down the screen, but when he released it, it shot right back up with a whir of springs. He exhaled sharply through his nose and pulled the screen down again. This time, he tied a wire at the base to a protruding screw driven directly into the dead display wall.

From his contemptuous snort, I knew Tsuros had ordered a subordinate to fix the latching mechanism, and they had failed. I would have given a great deal to watch the bumbling repairman catch hell.

The drills were careful to present a unified front, but I knew the truth. I could sometimes hear them bellowing at each other through the vents, like the lowing of distant beasts.

Tsuros went to dim the lights, but the rheostat didn't work. The lights only flickered. Another snort. Tsuros' jaw muscles bulged, the cords of his neck growing taut. I was nervous, and so were the others. Tsuros' anger was radioactive. If it breached containment, we might all catch a lethal dose.

There was a metal *click* as Tsuros whipped out a clasp knife. My hair stood on end. I was certain one of us was about to get gutted. Instead, Tsuros pried off the lighting control panel with the blade. I heard the *crack* of an electrical arc, then we were cast into darkness. I fought to keep from crying out. I didn't breathe until I heard the *clack* of the blade folding back into its handle.

Boots drummed across the darkened deck. I heard a switch flick, and then the projector's fan rattled and spun to life. The bulb warmed up, and I could see again. Tsuros cast a monstrous shadow as he passed before the projector screen. We hurried to line up in front of it at attention. I was too slow, I got stuck at the far left closest to Tsuros. It was always a bad idea to be within his arm's reach. To my right were Murderess, Liar, Corrupt, Addict, Glutton, then Pirate. The seven survivors.

Tsuros flipped the first transparency on the glass, then turned the knob. The silhouette of a spacecraft came into sharp focus. I recognized it immediately, a Clab SOCC.

"Pirate! Identify!"

Pirate hesitated. I clenched my jaw, trying to will the answer into his head.

"Collaborator Skysweeper Orbital Cleaning Craft, sir!" Pirate barked.

"What's the tonnage?" Tsuros pressed.

"No answer, sir!"

WHAP!

Tsuros slapped Pirate on the back of the neck. I kept my eyes straight at the screen. From the sound alone, I knew Tsuros had left a welt.

"CORRUPT! What is the tonnage of a Collaborator SOCC?"

"Fifty KT, sir!" Corrupt answered.

I steeled myself for the slap. He was off by an order of magnitude.

"WRONG!"

WHAP!

"MURDERESS!"

"No answer, sir!"

WHAP!

WHAP! That last one was Addict. Tsuros clocked him without even bothering to ask the question. Of course, they didn't know. We had no reason to know. The SOCC wasn't even a military craft. But for whatever reason, Tsuros was adamant we be able to identify every ship in the known universe within seconds. It made me wonder what in Diyu our mission could be. It was my turn in the crosshairs.

"Traitor, what is the tonnage of a Clab SOCC?"

"Sir! Five-point-five KT fueled, four-point-six dry."

"Correct! Traitor, how many reactors are in a VTS Frigate?"

"Ten in a standard frigate, sir! Eight turrets, one propulsion, and one backup! The Scorpion variant adds three reactors for the Stinger Plasma Projector for a total of thirteen!"

WHAP! He hit me hardest of all. The sound rippled through the others in a flinching wave and sparks danced in front of my eyes.

"Nobody likes a show-off, scum," Tsuros stage-whispered into my ringing ear.

"Yes, sir!" I shot back. My cheeks were ablaze. The others didn't understand that, for me, this was a reward. It hurt so good.

With boot steps as regular as a metronome, Tsuros returned to the projector. There was a tall stack of transparencies to plow through with multiple angles, partial occlusion, and colored diagrams. The questions came fast and furious today, and the reprisals were more vicious than ever.

Something was eating Tsuros, and it wasn't just the decrepit state of the classroom. The lesson went on for hours. Every time someone messed up, they would get hit. Two hours in, the others looked like they'd just lost a boxing match.

I never missed a question. I loved ships. My earliest memory was being held up to a porthole so I could watch a UNESECA freighter arriving. It was the biggest thing I'd ever seen. I remember the local transports hurrying out of its way, like sardines fleeing a whale.

It must have been my mother holding me up, but I can't remember anything about her. I was either two or three when she sold me. I like to imagine I bought her passage off Ring 5, that one of us made it out. But she probably just spent it all on drugs. Maybe she did the same thing over and over again, maybe I have brothers and sisters. I'll never know.

I didn't have money for contemporary media access, but the state-approved classics and vocational databases were all free. I used to collect repair manuals. I would pore over them for hours in my cubby until my cheap pad ran out of charge. My favorite thing to do was look at the exploded component view, and then try to visualize where each part was supposed to go. I loved assembling the ship piece by piece in my mind.

For the second time, I watched Murderess fail to distinguish between a Hezo AC-13 and a Clab Hari-77. It felt impossible she could keep screwing this up. The ships were superficially similar, both long-range scouts, about the same size and shape. But the Hari-77 was autonomous and had no armament. What looked like a canopy bubble was actually a sensor array.

For Murderess, the impossible was definitely possible. A dark purple line on her cheekbone from the blade of Tsuros' hand was proof. Corrupt's lip was split, and Addict had a mouse over his right eye. Pirate had a trickle of blood running down the side of his mouth through the un-plucked patches of his beard. He could remember the older ships perfectly, but he had trouble learning the newer ones.

One thing I'd noticed, there were no really new models of Collaborator ships. Everything we looked at was thirty or forty years old. I wondered if they'd run out of ideas, or if our ships didn't survive long enough to report on the new models.

Every muscle in my body ached from the tension as we reviewed the endless stack of transparencies. Over a certain timescale, the anticipation of pain is worse than the actual. I could enjoy it in the abstract, but it was nothing like the visceral immediacy of a fist in the eye.

The other inmates reeled, struggling to remain at attention. I wore the soldier's mask, but inside, I basked in their suffering. They hated the slides, hated Tsuros, hated me for being right. If only they knew how I exulted!

Tsuros put a slide on the screen, and his nose twitched. For a long time, he stared at the projection and didn't ask us anything. What the hell was he thinking? Whatever it was couldn't be good. His right hand curled into a fist. He turned his slitted eyes on me. My turn.

"Traitor!" Tsuros demanded.

"Sir! Collaborator AGA/LAG 81!"

"Role?"

"Dual role, interceptor-harrier, sir!"

"Deployment?"

"Glömer class carrier, sir!"

"Where were they first encountered?"

I froze, recognizing the trap. Officially, Da Jiao had been scrubbed from the Hezo Star Maps. The system had been classified. If I answered correctly, he could use my knowledge as a pretense to execute me. It would have been safer to feign ignorance. But Tsuros didn't need a pretense. I decided if I was going to die for this, I might as well go all the way and invoke the ancient, forbidden name.

"Arcturus."

I let my muscles go limp, expecting Tsuros to belt me immediately. But he surprised me and kicked me in the back of the knee. I hit the deck hard, and then he was on top of me, howling in my ear.

"YOU WILL ADDRESS ME AS SIR, INMATE!"

"YES, SIR!"

"NO SUCH STAR EXISTS! ARE YOU CLEAR ON THAT?"

"YES, SIR!"

He followed up with a wicked kick in my groin. I croaked and gasped, fighting back the urge to vomit. I couldn't spare the calories.

Tsuros stood in the projector beam. His face gleamed like a golden idol. An angry god, looking down on his creation with infinite disdain. Tsuros glared at the wobbly line of inmates, at the ruined light control panel dangling from the wall. His eyes lingered on the door, and his lower lip bulged as his tongue swept across his teeth. He turned back to the slide, inhaling deeply through his nostrils. He was making up his mind.

"Sit!" Tsuros commanded. The others moved towards the chairs lining the walls.

"No! On the floor with Traitor like the dogs you are."

The other inmates hastened to join me, stifling groans as they sank to the floor.

"Arcturus...," Tsuros trailed. He swept his hand towards the ship projected on the screen. We were looking at the top view, a titanium-white delta, with royal blue cheek blazes just below the canopy. The tips of her armament were crimson, twin front cannon, banked by linked polyphasic beams at center wing.

From the top view, her main weapon wasn't visible, but I knew what it was. A tri-catalyzed torpedo, roughly the same mass as the rest of the ship.

"Tell me about her, Traitor. How does she fight?"

"Sir! No answer!"

I honestly didn't know. Everything about Da Jiao was so heavily classified. I knew there had been a great battle at Usurus, and that it had been a turning point in the war, but I'd never been able to find footage or even a description of what had happened.

Tsuros jutted his lip with a superior nod. He turned back to the screen and gazed at the ship.

"The 81s are wasps. They issue from their carrier in a great angry swarm, shooting down incoming missiles and fighters. When the threat is neutralized, they go after the attacker. They fly in, dancing through flak, so close they can practically land on the target. Then they open up with the peelers, polyphasic beams. If they get through the hull, they lay their egg, a tri-cat torpedo. They buzz off, and then *BOOM!*"

Tsuros banged his fist on the projector table, making the image jump.

"*Hundan.* Our fighters couldn't touch them," Tsuros said, talking more to the screen than us. His eyes were focused on something far away, aflame with some ancient hate. Finally, he wheeled back on us.

"Arcturus is named from Arcas, the cursed hunter. He was turned into a bear, then imprisoned in the sky. The gods fixed his constellation above the horizon so he could never taste water again."

There was a long and painful silence. We didn't understand why Tsuros told us this.

"What really happened there, sir?" I dared. I was certain Tsuros would hit me again. I wanted it.

Tsuros turned to the squadron. There was something intolerable in his gaze. One by one, we broke. When he spoke again, his voice was low and even, stripped of all his customary theater.

"Get out of my sight, you dogs. Except you. Stay, Traitor," Tsuros ordered. My heart pounded. Tsuros had finally lost it, he was going to strangle me. I felt a pang of anguish in my bruised testicles and excitement singing in my temples.

At last.

When the others filed out, Tsuros brought two chairs, slamming one onto the deck beside me with a *bang* that made every cell in my body jump.

"Stand up."

I did so immediately, ignoring the pain in my groin. I stood ready to launch into attention or parade rest if either was ordered. But Tsuros didn't seem to care. He stared at me intently.

"I am going to tell you the legend of Arcturus. You are not to repeat a word to anyone. If you whisper one syllable of what I say, you will find yourself cast into the stars as well. Am I clear?"

"Yes, sir!"

"My curse is more than just thirst, Traitor. I will fire up a crucible and make you my Vazul. Surely, a freak like you knows the story?"

"Yes, sir!"

"Refresh my memory, inmate!"

"Vászoly of Nyitra, sir! Grand Prince of the Hungarians. Abducted by his cousin, King Stephen I. Abacinated and deafened with molten lead so he would be unfit to rule. Died in 1032."

"Excellent, inmate. But that's nothing compared to my wrath. You won't see the airlock for years. I will flay you until your entire body is a single, shrieking, exposed nerve. You will be shackled in the burn ward, hooked up to life support. Flame imperishable, a being of pure pain. You will beg to die for *years* before I give you to the void. Do you understand me?"

"Yes, sir!" I replied. I tried not to wince from the swelling pain in my crotch. Tsuros was a hell of a drill. He had every hair on my body standing at attention.

"Sit," he commanded.

Tsuros took the chair beside the projector. We sat facing the screen as if we were watching a movie together. Tsuros would throw on a transparency whenever he mentioned a ship, pointing out the strengths and weaknesses of each. He told me the idiosyncrasies of each design, the tactics he'd seen each employ. I drank in every word.

With me, Tsuros could get into a level of detail that would have been wasted on the others. All the information I'd been able to amass as a civilian was just a thin outline compared to what he knew. Tsuros spoke as if he'd fought with or against nearly every ship that had flown for the last century. Perhaps he had. I began to wonder what Tsuros' real rank was. He knew far more than a sergeant had any right to.

While the rest of the flight scrubbed toilets, I reveled in the legend of Arcturus. It was as if Tsuros had composed it just for me. The legend had everything I wanted. Spaceships! Secrets! History, hubris, human misery! The best part was the oath of secrecy. With every breath, absolute suffering loomed over me, like an executioner's axe.

I felt so alive, and so afraid. The threat to flay me was no bluff. Tsuros was the devil himself. He knew exactly how my gears turned, and he would wind them until something snapped. Rung by rung, ring by ring, he dragged me deeper into the pit.

What was at the bottom?

王濬楼船下益州
金陵王气黯然收
千寻铁锁沈江底
一片降旛出石头
人世几回伤往事
山形依旧枕寒流
从今四海为家日
故垒萧萧芦荻秋

6
THE LEGEND OF ARCTURUS

"It was a long, long time ago, Traitor. The Navy was different then. We thought we were pure enough to wield the devil's weapons without becoming demons ourselves. What a price we paid! The Hezo Collective Prosperity Sphere was young and wild, heady off a string of victories that seemed never-ending. We'd yet to accept the inevitability of entropy."

Tsuros gestured around to the various inept repairs. His eyes lifted to the rusting bolts in the ceiling.

"Look around you! Everything falls apart. Back then, if you'd told me I would be drilling a herd of incompetent convicts in some dilapidated VTS shit-hulk, I would have laughed in your face. Then I would have knocked your fucking teeth out. Yet, here we are. What brought us here?"

In my case, a JDM prisoner barge. Tsuros probably arrived in a Yun-Zitanwon carrier. Luckily, I realized his question was rhetorical before I could blurt out an answer. My mind was still in silhouette training mode.

"*Weakness,* Traitor. Since we left the trees, one enemy has defeated all of our greatest leaders and toppled our mightiest empires. *Degeneration.* Sinister whispers that the weak would be strong, if only life were fair! Misfits must be included! The aberrant must be tolerated! The steadfast ought to feed the slothful! Time and time again, when the war is won, the meek rise up to swallow the weary victors. The result is inevitable. Chaos. Confusion. Discord. Bureaucracy. Aftermath.

"Before the fall, the Hezo claimed a hundred systems, and we had eyes on a thousand more. I served Z-Admiral Tong Lang Chinci in Strike Force Liu. Think of the Hezo's greatest victories: Teegarden, Epsilon Indi, Ran. What fleet spearheaded them all? You know the name, say it!"

"Steel Wave, sir!" I barked on command.

"That's right, inmate. Steel Wave."

Tsuros threw a register of ships onto the projector, Steel Wave at its height. I immediately recognized mark III battleships, *Zhanwu* carriers, and a VTS ultra-dreadnaught. There were also a few classes of ships I had never seen before, the bottom of the sheet was stamped with a *mi* classification. I was dying to know more, but I kept my mouth shut.

"The bloodiest enterprise in human history. We swept through Collaborator systems, crimson in our wake! Planets evacuated if we so much as glanced in their direction. Admiral Chinci understood the basic truth of the Clabs. It wasn't enough to defeat them. They had to be eradicated.

"Decades of battle led to the Eye of Dagon. In that smoldering disc, we charged directly into the collaborator fortifications. Steel Wave never crested. When the day was done, Fomalhaut Fortress lay in ruins, and the backbone of the Collaborators was broken forevermore. They would never again field the grand fleets we battled at Curve Array and the Celestial Spear. Our boot came down, and the cockroaches scattered to the stars!"

A smile had crept onto my face. I caught myself and jolted back into military bearing. Any show of emotion usually meant I'd be struck, but not today. Tsuros let it slide, looser than I'd ever seen him before. When he spoke of the old battles, his eyes blazed with a lurid incandescence.

"Steel Wave fought the longest. We were frontline in all the pivotal battles, and we took the most grievous casualties. Still, the work of finishing the war fell to us. The other fleets returned home to victory parades. They settled down, got fat, and raised families. Our hands stayed bloody. We knew what had to be done.

"System by system, we hunted down the cowards and put them to the knife. There was much work to be done, and we had the stomach for it. We were good at it. If we'd been left alone, there wouldn't have been two Collaborators left in the galaxy to conspire together."

Tsuros shook his head with regret.

"But you're sitting here. You know that wasn't to be. People forget, Traitor. When the danger is passed, they love to puff themselves up and pretend they were never frightened. After the great rout at Fomalhaut, everything changed.

"High Command was eager to shift away from the austerity of total war. A new class of soft-bellied usurpers rose, eager to reap what Steel Wave had sown. They had no use for warriors who would not compromise or relent. We were an obstacle to their schemes, and they feared us. Our teeth were still sharp."

"High Command sent Steel Wave to the most distant posts, far away from their schemes. The outcome was inevitable. Without our voices on the council, there was no one to quell their idiotic ideas. After all of our valor, all of our sacrifice, we handed over the reins to a pack of squabbling children!

"Understand this—the Collaborators were not finished! The wound we inflicted at Dagon was grievous but not mortal. No military can afford to be of two minds in a war. Collaborator vermin will rise, again and again.

"The civilians could never understand this. A new faction rose, administrators and bureaucrats who traded empty promises for power. They called themselves Reconcilers. They spoke of the need for unity, the imminence of peace. The fools had the masses convinced the Collaborators would surrender if only Steel Wave would stop killing them. They whined that our assaults damaged infrastructure, our purges liquidated labor pools."

I struggled to process this. I was a child when Keilu capitulated to the Hezo Collective Prosperity Sphere. I couldn't even remember a time when they weren't in charge of every aspect of my life. They were a monolith, a star-spanning bureaucracy too vast to even dream of opposing. Tsuros spoke of them like a pack of squabbling children, no better than Corrupt and Liar fighting over whose turn it was on chute duty. I had never even heard of the Reconcilers. All mention of them had been purged.

"The Reconcilers were swine, filth who never fought, never flew a mission! Yet, there were plenty of cowards and cripples to glom onto their stupid ideas. There are always more worms than warriors. As we hunted in the wilderness, their corruption spread. The constant combat kept us pure. Steel Wave was Absolutist to the core. Do you know what Absolutist means? It means the only good Clab is a dead Clab. Collaboration is a cancer, and every infected cell must be purged. Tolerance is treason!"

My eyes were locked on Tsuros' right fist, watching it shake with each point. He could turn on me in an instant. Instead, he rose to his feet, and paced across the projector beam as he spoke.

"Admiral Tong Lang Chinci was as constant as caesium. Steel Wave never relented, discipline and morale never wavered. If we'd had just one more like her, you and I would have never met. You would have never been born. That vile nest of sympathizers that spawned you would have been purged with fire."

Silently, I wished it had. I never asked for this. Tsuros prodded at me, unwilling to let me wallow.

"Tell me something, Traitor, what's the rarest element in the universe?"

"Astatine, sir!"

"Not astatine, you literal-minded fool. It's leadership. Great leaders are the rarest element in the universe. We're lucky to see one a century. The Hezo squandered their conquering empress. Tong Lang Chinci spent years in null-space, sweeping from star to star as an exterminator."

Tsuros threw a transparency on the screen that read *STEEL WAVE - WILDERNESS CAMPAIGN* at the top. The left side was a star map where the cyclonic path of Steel Wave had been rendered as a numbered sequence of arrows. There were hundreds of them. Diverging lines indicated splits into wings which hit multiple targets simultaneously.

The right side of the sheet was a table. The first column was titled *CLAB BASES*. Stretching to the bottom of the sheet was a long list of planets I had never heard of before. The next column was titled *PURGED*. A date was listed for each planet.

I squinted at the figures. Obviously this had to be some mistake. My eyes darted from the orderly list of planets to the sprawling warpath. *Purged*, not defeated. I was in free-fall, terrified to look down. They were just numbers. The transparency was a prop in Tsuros' fable.

Tsuros rapped a finger on the glass, snapping my attention to the next sheet. It was an org chart of the High Command with Reconciler name printed in red. Just like the dead planets, I had never heard of any of them.

"See how the Reconcilers consolidated their power while we were occupied? It's the great tragedy of politics, competent people are too busy actually producing to bother with bureaucracy. Governance is the province of the inept."

Tsuros paused to gauge my response to what he'd just shown me. The stakes had changed. This was nothing like the way the other drills watched me suffer in dead-eyed detachment. Tsuros was *invested*. He was animated and eager, an electric newness to his words like it was the first time he'd told anyone.

This was no fable.

The station creaked around us as I fought back the urge to scream. A series of clangs reverberated through the vents, then I could hear distant cursing.

"The grid closet," I blurted, recognizing the particular timbre of the impacts. The hatch of the electrical distribution closet was almost impossible to pry open. The insulating gel had swollen with age. Desperate for any diversion, I wondered what had broken.

Tsuros snapped his fingers. My mouth clapped shut like a magic trick.

"Our surroundings are temporary and irrelevant. Only the objective matters. Focus!"

Tsuros threw another sheet up, a chart that showed the intervals of Steel Wave's resupplies and reinforcements. Tsuros snapped a finger on a spot where the steady ticks developed an arrythmia that worsened with time.

"Here's where they gain power. The Reconciler cowards realized we would never lose our edge, but they didn't dare oppose us directly. There was no need. Time is the ally of decay. The right course is never popular. The media turned, smearing shit on the heroes they'd once spangled with glory. Subterfuge was everywhere. Our orders were jumbled, our supply trains were disrupted. We arrived at systems only to find the Collaborators had fled. Someone in High Command was leaking."

"The captains of Steel Wave advised Admiral Chinci to lead a delegation to Sigma Draconis and throw our hat into the political ring before it was too late. The Reconciler dogs wouldn't be so quick to laugh if we were in striking range.

"Admiral Chinci refused to sully herself in that pit of snakes. Instead, she announced a great reorganization of the fleet to make us more agile and more self-sufficient. After the great shake-up, she filed a battle plan with High Command for an all-out attack on the Collaborator infestation at Barnard's Star. Once more, the Collaborators were warned. Our ships arrived to find the system deserted."

A wicked grin cracked Tsuros' face, filling me with expectant fear.

"Strangely, only two ships arrived at Barnard's Star that day. They were *Ta Bing* and *Despicable*. It must have seemed an odd pairing for an assault. *Despicable* was a top-of-the-line Mark VI Jiangan Destroyer. *Ta Bing* was the oldest destroyer in the fleet. Minutes after arrival, *Ta Bing* suffered catastrophic engine failure. Her captain broadcast a distress call. The captain of *Despicable* answered by powering up his main cannons."

"If only I could have been there," Tsuros lamented. "I would die one thousand deaths just to see the looks on their faces. All the Reconciler sympathizers and High Command moles, every turncoat in the fleet had been reassigned to the *Ta Bing*. The guns of *Despicable* were their firing squad!"

Tsuros raised a fist in triumph. His laugh was coarse and cruel. I was so caught in his story, I almost fucked up and laughed along. Tsuros' face was livid with a hate that had burned for decades.

"*Sic semper proditores*," Tsuros spat, staring at me.

"*Fiat justitia ruat caelum*," I dared to agree.

Tsuros blinked at my outburst. His eyes rolled from his fist to my face. I was hungry for it, anything to blot out those terrible figures. He wanted to beat me, and I needed to be beaten. But Tsuros saw right through me.

"If you only knew how right you are. That will be all for today. Dismissed." He pointed at the door.

No! He couldn't leave me like this. I was in ruins.

"You want the rest of the story, inmate?" Tsuros taunted, leaning in close. I could see my reflection in his eyes. I gazed at him with the arrant submission of a begging dog.

"Yes sir," I rasped.

"I know you do. I know what you are, Traitor. You're weak. Spineless and afraid, with a head full of heresy. You think you're at the bottom? I've barely begun. I will hammer you flat! I'll knock the slag off your rotten soul. From this worthless scrap, I'll make something new, pure with purpose.

Raw, gleaming steel, aimed at the heart of our adversary. Are you ready?"

"Yes sir," I whispered, flush with desire.

"No more doubts. No more holding back. Get those scores up. Bury the other inmates."

Tsuros dismissed me. I limped back to the barracks, aching with every step.

死別已吞聲
生別常惻惻
江南瘴癘地
逐客無消息
故人入我夢
明我長相憶
君今在羅網
何以有羽翼
恐非平生魂
路遠不可測
魂來楓林青
魂返關塞黑
落月滿屋梁
猶疑照顏色
水深波浪闊
無使蛟龍得

7
THE SIXTH CIRCLE

I dreamed of a foundry, a vast grid of blackened walkways suspended across a scalding *sesto cerchio* of smoking pits. Poisonous plumes of sparks spiraled above hectares of glowing crucibles. I stood at the controls above a shimmering vat of molten lead. The gangway rumbled beneath my feet as galena gnashed in the teeth of distant giants. The walls of this place were the tuyeres of a blast furnace, they groaned as if some mad organist was playing the pipes. The panel was a confusing jumble of dials, levers, dip switches, and flashing buttons. The instructions were engraved in blackletter on a steel plate, eight dicta. When I tried to read them, the letters slithered into an inscrutable mess.

"Traitor!" hissed a voice in the darkness.

Shadows dangled above the pit. I threw a heavy knife switch, the circuit activated with a loud *CLACK!* Harsh spotlights burned overhead.

They'd all been hanged.

The other inmates swayed in the rising heat with chains wound around their necks. Their bodies had a charnel gradient, legs black and bloated, upper bodies pale and bloodless. Only Murderess survived. She dug her fingers beneath the noose and fought for every breath. Sweat bled from her naked body. The drops hissed and spat as they skittered across the searing lead.

"HELP ME!" Murderess begged. Her legs kicked as she clawed at the steel noose. High above us, the pulley clinked to life. Link by link, she sank towards the vat. I searched the panel for a way to save her. There were so many buttons, I didn't know which to press.

"*Please!*" she gasped. The more she struggled, the tighter the noose wound.

I mashed a flashing red button. With a gear-grinding screech the chain lurched to a stop. I rushed to the rail, reaching out a hand but she was too far.

High above, there was a delicate *ping*, and the chain whirred. With a shriek, Murderess plunged into the molten lead.

The vat roared static like a deep fryer, heaving globs of boiling lead that exploded like grenades. Murderess's last, flailing movement whipped through the chain in a wave, then it was taut again. The silvery surface of the pool was bubbling with indigestion, pools of dark blood were foaming and boiling off. It was all my fault.

The furnace pipes belched twelve bass strokes to greet midnight. The pitch swelled to a mocking scordatura tritone and the chain clinked upward, dappled with shining solder-beads. There was nothing left of Murderess but a skeleton. Her electroplated bones gleamed and seemed to dance as the chain reeled her up. I was eye-to-socket with the chromed skull. The jaw creaked open.

"Traitor!"

I woke with a cry. Someone was shaking me. I tried to bat them away, but my arms had no strength. I was soaked in sweat.

"Traitor!" The voice urged again, in a low whisper. It was Pirate.

The dream stubbornly refused to fade. The red lights of the barracks were flickering like the forge. I was afraid to look up at Pirate, certain I'd find a bloodless corpse.

"You were screaming," he explained.

I forced myself to sit up. Pirate was worried. Screamers got locked. The ones in my first training flight were all gone within a month.

"What did he do to you?" Pirate asked.

"Vászoly," I muttered. Pirate didn't get it and I was too upset to explain. I tried to poke holes in the nightmare, rationalizing that a body wouldn't sink in lead like that. It didn't help.

"Do you want to talk about it?" Pirate offered. He kept his voice low. His eyes darted to the door. If a drill burst in, he was done for. The other inmates had the good sense to pretend to be asleep.

The strange melody was stuck in my head. I realized I was really hearing it. The sound was barely audible.

"What is that?" I asked.

Pirate was too old to hear the music. I padded towards the latrine, searching for the source. Unexpectedly, Pirate followed me in. The sound was coming from the vent over the toilet, where I'd stashed my emergency rations. I climbed onto the bowl and listened to the distant notes.

"Careful!" Pirate hissed sharply. "If the drills come, you're dead!"

"There's music," I said, ignoring his concern. It wasn't like Pirate to be so anxious, Tsuros must have hit him harder than I thought.

"Listen," I offered, climbing down.

Pirate looked uneasy, but he couldn't resist his curiosity. He climbed up and bent his ear to the vent.

"I hear it," he whispered.

"What is that?" I asked. Someone was committing a crime. Anything that could reproduce music had been forbidden.

"*Danse Macabre*."

"Huh?"

"From old Earth. Saint-Saëns," Pirate said quietly. "You wouldn't know it. The Hezo purged it all."

I knew more than I let on, but not this. We lingered in the stall, listening to the haunting tones until our courage ran out. I couldn't place the instrument. The notes were too thin for a piano, too fast for a harp. I was glad Pirate heard it too, so I didn't think I was going crazy. As we crept back to our bunks, he clapped me on the shoulder.

"Only a dream," he assured me.

"Thank you," I whispered, sincerely grateful. He didn't have to help me like this. Pirate could have feigned sleep like the others, and let the drills drag me away. I vowed to remember his kindness.

Sleep was impossible. I stared at the ceiling through the slats of the vacant bunk above me. I strained to hear through the slumbering prisoners, but the dance had ended. Restless, I turned towards Murderess's bunk. The crimson light flashed in her eyes.

She was awake and staring at me.

I choked back a scream.

猿鸟犹疑畏简书
风云常为护储胥
徒令上将挥神笔
终见降王走传车
管乐有才原不忝
关张无命欲何如
他年锦里经祠庙
梁父吟成恨有余

8
THE LEGEND OF ARCTURUS II

Tsuros was hung over.

I don't think the other inmates could tell. Bloodshot eyes and a short temper? That was Tsuros every day. His uniform was impeccable as always. No whiff of liquor could escape that aura of soap and starch. I only noticed when he was still. There was a dreamy linger in his gaze and a new depth in his glower. He couldn't sleep either. Behind that troubled brow, Steel Wave rode again.

The projector was waiting for us in the classroom. Murderess flinched when she saw it. Normally, silhouette trainings were spaced out to give us time to heal. The classroom lights were working again, and the screen was rolled down without the tether. Some poor engineer had caught hell. It pleased me to know everyone was suffering. But my schadenfreude was short-lived.

"Lucky day, inmates. Lucky day!" Tsuros boomed. He clapped his hands together in mock-excitement. Dread rippled up the line.

"I had a revelation this morning! I was watching you apes fumble through flight training, astounded that Corrupt somehow managed to strike three static pylons. Three! Is that a squadron record?"

It wasn't, Murderess had hit four the week before. Still, three was too many. Corrupt struggled to stand. The impact contractions had nearly crushed him.

"As I watched that sad farce, *Jué wù* struck. I realized for the first time just how generous the HCPS Navy truly is! In spite of your monumental ineptitude, they have accommodated each of you with your very own bunk and footlocker. To me, this seems extravagant! I'm a frugal man. If it were up to me, you would all be housed in deep space at no cost whatsoever."

Tsuros paced behind us as we stared forward at the projector screen, locked in rigid attention. I stopped breathing as his boots drew close to me. Someone was about to get nailed and I hoped it was me.

Instead, Corrupt swayed at the end of the line. Tsuros snuck up behind him. I hated that. The sound of Tsuros' boots was a fundamental constant of this place. When he moved silently, it felt like cheating.

Tsuros set a hand between Corrupt's shoulder blades and shoved. Corrupt pitched forward and banged his knees on the deck. It had to hurt like hell, but he sprang to his feet and back to attention at once. Tsuros resumed pacing.

"Yes inmates, the navy is indeed magnanimous! I decided to take a stroll through the barracks, to see how appreciative you all are! I expected to find them immaculate!"

The heavy steps continued, ticking down to our doom. Tsuros halted directly behind me.

"Imagine my disappointment."

Tsuros slammed his fist into the back of my head. My vision went black, my eardrums rang like cymbals. I clenched my jaw, fighting to stay on my feet. If I went down, I wasn't getting back up. My cheeks burned.

I deserve this.

Tsuros continued down the line, belting each inmate. *WHAM!* He hit Pirate. *WHAM!* Murderess. Corrupt was at the very end of the line. I tensed up, stifling a suicidal urge to cry *NO!* I was afraid the blow would kill him.

WHAM!

Tsuros didn't pull his punch. If anything, he hit Corrupt harder than the rest of us. Corrupt was unconscious before his head hit the deck.

"Pubic hairs! Bloodstains! Scabs! Every bunk except one was filthy! The place was a fucking pigsty! How can you live like that? You disgust me!" Tsuros howled.

How? I knew the others were wondering the same thing. Every morning, we rushed to make the barracks spotless before flight training. How could we have missed so much? Either Tsuros was lying or someone sabotaged us.

"You two! Drag this trash to the refuse chute."

Tsuros thrust the sign of the horns at Murderess and Liar then jabbed his thumb at Corrupt's body. They hurried over and grabbed Corrupt's arms and legs.

"Sir, he's breathing!" Liar said.

I sucked air through my teeth. It was impossibly brave of Liar to speak up while Tsuros was doling out punishment. Tsuros stared at Liar, I was afraid we'd be dragging him to the chute too. But Tsuros surprised me.

"Then take him to the infirmary instead, idiot. Double-time. Afterward you are to proceed immediately to waste reclamation and get suited up with the others. Since you ingrates want to live like swine, you can spend the rest of the day wallowing in shit. If you are unable to complete quarterly tank maintenance before 2000 hours, you will spend the night in there. Do you understand?"

"Yes, sir!"

"DISMISSED!"

I moved towards the door with the others. The back of my head pounded with every step. My mind raced ahead of the pain, trying to figure out how we could clean the Augean waste reclamation tanks before 2000 hours without Corrupt.

It was a two-day job to get them cleaned and cycled.

"Traitor!" Tsuros barked, breaking my stride.

"Yes, sir?"

"Where the fuck do you think you're going? Your bunk was clean. Sit down."

He pointed at the chairs beside the projector. Murderess looked up from Corrupt. Her face contorted with hate.

Oh no.

I slumped into the chair as they picked up Corrupt and carried him away. I was stunned at what Tsuros had done to me. He'd set it all up so the others would blame me.

I was supremely fucked.

Tsuros killed the lights and strutted over to the projector.

"Now, where were we?" Tsuros asked, grinning like a fiend.

"*Despicable*, sir," I said.

"Don't get clever with me," he warned. "I can stick you with the shit-squad."

I almost asked him to.

"Or with Corrupt," Tsuros added, reading it in my face.

There was never a choice. I swallowed and faced the screen. Tsuros had a fresh stack of transparencies prepared.

"The rats on Ta Bing drowned in a rain of shells. Unbeknownst to High Command, Admiral Chinci executed a surprise attack against EZ Aquarii. This time, the Collaborators had no advance warning."

Tsuros put the first sheet on the glass, a battle map. Steel Wave thrust towards Sanguinus as Collaborators converged on them from all directions. He took a deep breath and stared at the map for a few moments, savoring the memory.

"You should have seen it, Traitor! The battle of Hydroparastatae was a slaughter like no other. The Clabs came at us like madmen, sacrificing themselves in droves to slow our advance. We penetrated their lines and found what they were so desperate to protect. Hidden in the shadow of Sanguinus was the gravity signature of a massive ship. We were hot to chase, but it was impossibly fast. The ship escaped into null-space before we made visual contact. The rest of the Clabs tried to flee, but it was too late for most. When the dust settled, there were barely any survivors left to interrogate. From those few, we pried a name for the Collaborator superweapon. They called it the *Titan Forge*."

Collaborator superweapon? I forgot all about my aching head.

"Hydroparastatae was our anagnorisis. At last, we had proof of the traitors in High Command. Some of Chinci's captains argued we should ignore the *Titan Forge*, fly to Sigma Draconis, and seize control of the empire."

Tsuros paused, biting back something he'd been about to say. I didn't dare ask if he was one of those captains.

"Admiral Tong Lang Chinci balked at the Rubicon. Perhaps it was duty, perhaps it was honor. I think she simply couldn't resist hunting the greatest whale of all time. *Iacta alea est.*

"We chased the *Titan Forge* deep into Collaborator space, beset at every step by traps and ambushes. The Clabs continued their harried construction as they fled, devouring asteroid belts and drinking deep from nebulae. After months of pursuit, we finally caught up with them at the Wolf 497 Anomaly. It was our first look at the beast."

Tsuros placed a illustration of the *Titan Forge* on the glass. It was huge! The Zhanwu carrier drawn next to it for scale looked like an ant. The *Titan Forge* resembled a silver moringa seed, eighty kilometers in diameter. At the bottom right corner of the sheet, a classification was stamped. *Three mi.* I could be executed just for viewing this, if I wasn't already condemned. Tsuros swapped to an isometric representation where arrows showed three pieces of an outer shell orbiting the *Forge*.

"These are a trigonal hosahedron of free-floating lune. Incubators. They constantly bombarded the core with gamma radiation. It's difficult to tell on this 2D representation, but each of these has an independent orbit."

"What happens when lune overlap?" I asked.

"It amplifies their output. When two lune overlap, they flood space with pions and neutrinos. We witnessed only one triple stack. It created an exponential increase. The discharge was intense enough to burn out sensors twenty thousand kilometers away."

I stared at the image and wondered how the hell it could generate that kind of power.

"In addition to incubating the core, the lune were also the propulsion source for the *Forge*. They were the first examples of radiative plane projection. The great-grandfather of the RAMP system in your ships. At the time, Steel Wave had nothing that could match it. This behemoth could outrun our swiftest ships."

The next transparency was a series of measurements and equations. I puzzled at them, but the math was far beyond me.

"I'll summarize," Tsuros said, reading my confusion. "The mass of the *Titan Forge* is far, far greater than it should be. There are three possible conclusions. One, our instruments were malfunctioning or compromised. Two, the Collaborators have some kind of space-bending technology. Three, they found a way to collect matter from a *neutron star*."

Impossible. Tsuros had to be bullshitting me.

"Believe it, Traitor. If permitted, I have no doubt the *Titan Forge* could have annihilated every ship in our fleet. But like all the works of the Devil, the ancient shackles hold. The *Forge* had no choice but to retreat, outrunning our missiles and escaping into null-space. Just as Admiral Chinci anticipated.

"She had split Steel Wave into three attack wings, Alpha, Beta, and Gamma. Alpha's task was to surprise the *Forge* at Wolf 497 and flush it into retreat. Beta and Gamma wings waited in ambush at the two closest systems. Gambling that Murfid was the most likely escape vector, Chinci assigned her most powerful artillery to Gamma wing and took direct command.

"Chinci won her bet. The *Titan Forge* emerged from null-space at Murfid with shields down and defenses offline. The behemoth was greeted by a furious barrage from all sides. The *Titan Forge* was incredible, not invincible."

Tsuros placed the transparency I'd been waiting for, The Mark I Hyperion Hyperlauncher. I devoured every detail. Nine tubes arranged in a ring around a central magazine, twice as long the main ship body. Each tube had a dedicated four-man gunner team. There were 134 engineers on board, more than many capital ships required. The design was wildly complex, there were twenty reactors, two for every tube, one primary, and one propulsion. It reminded me of a gatling gun.

"Our surprise attack destroyed the outermost lune. The second lune was damaged so badly the *Forge* had to abandon it. Several hyperlauncher torpedoes made their way to the seed-core, bursting like solar flares. All the firepower we could muster was not enough. The *Forge* was able to raise her shields and limp away to Arcturus."

"Once more, the history of mankind pivoted on Admiral Chinci. Alpha Wing and Beta Wing were too distant to join us in time. Arcturus was a Collaborator stronghold. Chinci would have to fight with a third of her fleet or risk the *Forge* escaping again.

"Admiral Chinci chose to pursue. Our call for emergency reinforcements was answered by S-Admiral Xishi. Strike Force San was close to a ringship. They would be able to join our attack. Xishi requested we delay and prepare for a joint assault, but there was blood in the water and Chinci would not be denied."

Tsuros placed a transparency entitled "ASSAULT ON ARCTURUS–GAMMA WING." My eyes leapt to another unknown ship type. Tsuros tapped his finger on the illustration.

"*Reciprocity,* the very first Wusexikai Shield Battery to see combat. We had just one Zhanwu Carrier, two Mark III battleships, five frigates, and the Hyperion hyperlauncher. Admiral Chinci had the helm at her flagship, *Bulldog.* The last operational VTS Ultra-Dreadnaught."

The next transparency was marked ASSAULT ON ARCTURUS–COLLABORATOR DEFENSES. The entire sheet was filled with Collaborator ships and defensive structures. I could barely sit still. This was the stuff of legends! Tsuros grinned at me.

"We stormed into Arcturus. The Clabs outnumbered us three to one, but we were Steel Wave! We carved a bloody road through the defenders, hell-bent on our quarry. The *Forge* cowered in the shadow of Ursurus, docked at the outermost orbital ring for emergency repairs. As we battled our way across the system, the first waves of Strike Force San emerged from null-space at our rear."

The next transparency was Strike Force San.

"Shangjiang Xishi's fleet boasted three Zhanwu Carriers, Two Guandao Missile Frigates, and five Mark V battleships. Xishi arrived last, in command of the *Shunian*, a prototype Mark VII battleship."

Shunian was gigantic. The flagship was double the size of later production Mark VIIs. I would have loved to pore over a full schematic, but Tsuros was moving ahead rapidly.

"Xishi broadcast orders for Gamma Wing to hold position and wait for Strike Force San. We could not comply. We were too deeply committed to slow our advance. We reached the Roche limit of Ursurus, audaciously poised within range of their planetary defense array. The Clabs must have thought we'd gone mad!"

"While the Ursurians were preparing to fire, Admiral Chinci demanded the immediate and unconditional surrender of all Collaborator forces in the system. I can still remember the fire in her eyes, the murder in her smile! Tong Lang Chinci, the Angel of Death!"

Tsuros banged his fist against the projector for emphasis.

I jolted in my seat.

"There were no white flags from the Collaborators. They knew all about Steel Wave. They answered our demand with a T-GZK burst, one of the most horrific weapons ever devised. The battle could have ended right there, with every living organism in Gamma Wing sterilized. But the Collaborators didn't know about *Reciprocity*. The Wusexikai Shield Battery detected the hypernova formation and activated. It drank in the incredible energies flung at our fleet and reflected them back at their source. Can you imagine it?"

I shook my head.

"Neither could the Clabs. Before that day, no military had ever deployed T-GZK weaponry against an inhabited planet. It was too barbaric even for the VTS. The Ursurian fools were the first, with their unwitting act of self-genocide. The reflected burst caused a mass-extinction event across the entire hemisphere. A billion collaborators died in a single shot."

I could only blink at the screen. *A billion!*

"We had no choice but to return fire. Our answering barrage destroyed all three of Ursurus' orbital rings. On the far side of the planet, the survivors awoke to find the sky ablaze. The three great bands that spanned their horizons shattered. They fell in a cataclysmic rain. It will persist for centuries. Ursurus was once the busiest shipyard in Collaborator space. Today, it is an irradiated graveyard. In fifty thousand years, the planet will still be uninhabitable."

I drew my head back from the idea. Tsuros pressed on, twisting the knife.

"This is the work of the Collaborators. They will make any sacrifice for their demon god. They will martyr planets, snuff entire systems. They would slit this galaxy's throat to bloody his altar. This is what you're fighting against! The Clabs could have surrendered, but they chose planetary suicide."

He threw a picture of Ursurus on the projector. The planet was dark and cratered, the space around it buzzed with debris that had not yet spun into a ring.

"Even the total destruction of a Ursurus was not enough to convince the Collaborators to relinquish *Titan Forge*. There was great chaos in the aftermath. Some of the Collaborator wings fired wildly, some were motionless. Civilian ships scrambled from all over the system, flying at us on collision courses. Freighters, tankers, transports, miners, we swatted them down like flies while they sacrificed themselves to slow our advance. It felt like Hydroparastatae all over again. Ahead of us, the Collaborators rallied for a final defense. We surged forward, eager for another shot at the *Forge*.

"In all of this, we'd nearly forgotten Strike Force San at our rear. We received an emergency transmission from the *Shunian*. Shangjiang Xishi appeared on our coms. He was pale and shaken."

A sheet with Xishi's portrait cracked onto the projector, side by side with Tong Lang Chinci's. The contrast was stark. Xishi's face was a ruin of involute sags. Chinci's lines were sharp enough to draw blood. I saw what Tsuros meant. The woman was a weapon. Tsuros' eyes lingered on the screen before he moved to the next sheet.

```
TRANSCRIPT - SJ XISHI - ZJ CHINCI

ARCTURUS - 5217:08:23:0414 - 3MI


SJ XISHI: ADMIRAL CHINCI! WHAT HAVE YOU DONE?

ZJ CHINCI: I WAS FIRED UPON, SHANGJIANG. I RETALIATED

SJ XISHI: YOU'VE KILLED THEM ALL!

ZJ CHINCI: NOT YET, SIR. BUT I WILL.

*SJ XISHI TRANSMISSION INTERRUPTED*
```

Tsuros pointed to the interruption.

"This is when Xishi's side of the screen locked up. That withered old face was frozen in an expression of fathomless disgust. Behind us, we saw Strike Force San begin to maneuver. He was giving orders off-air."

ZJ CHINCI: ALL UNITS, EXECUTE PLAN FOUR

SJ XISHI TRASMISSION RESUMED

SJ XISHI: ADMIRAL TONG LANG CHINCI. YOU HAVE COMMITTED CRIMES

AGAINST HUMANITY. YOU ARE RELIEVED OF DUTY. CEASE PURSUIT AND

STAND DOWN.

ZJ CHINCI: ALL UNITS! SHANGJIANG XISHI IS A COLLABORATOR

SYMPATHIZER. HE HAS BETRAYED THE NAVY! I AM ASSUMING DIRECT

COMMAND OF STRIKE FORCE SAN. ANY WHO OPPOSE ME WILL BE

DESTROYED!

SJ XISHI: YOU FOOL! YOU'RE SURROUNDED! STAND DOWN OR-

TRANSMISSION ENDS

Sergeant Tsuros rapped his finger on the final line.

"Xishi's voice vanished in thunder. How can I describe it? It was like Mahler's tenth symphony. *Shunian* had nine reactors on her starboard side. The Hyperion hyperlauncher played a *schreckliche* chord upon them. *Sforzando!* Nine null-space torpedoes, synchronized to the picosecond! Fired before Xishi even gave the order to stand down. Chinci knew! *Der Teufel tanzt es mit mir!"*

Tsuros' eyes blazed with malevolence in the projector light. The next sheet showed Strike Force San's capital ships packed into a tight formation.

"In those days, Hezo Battle Protocol dictated the command detachment should fly in close formation. They huddled together to benefit from the excellent protection of their Wugui Shield Battery. It was an effective strategy against the Collaborators. Few of their weapons could penetrate the telluric particle shell.

"But we weren't Collaborators! Our hyperlauncher torpedoes phased right through the shell, directly into *Shunian's* reactors. They exploded in blooms of relativistic shearing like razor chrysanthemums. *Shunian* was annihilated in a single volley! A terrible chain reaction began."

Tsuros took out his red pen, drawing arrows radiating out from *Shunian.*

"Nearby was the *Quanto,* a Guandao missile frigate commanded by Zhongjiang Ding Yahno. At first, it seemed she might weather the explosion, but a fire ignited in her magazine. Fifteen seconds later she was consumed by a massive eruption. Her sister ship *Minbing* and reserve Zhanwu *Glia* were dragged down to Diyu with her. In a single stroke, Strike Force San had lost their Shangjiang, their Zhongjiang, and both of their main artillery!"

When Tsuros finished drawing, the sheet looked like a diagram of a fusion reaction. *What a shot!*

"*Audentis Fortuna iuvat!* Learn that well, *proditor.* Strike fast, strike first! Without Chinci's audacious attack, neither of us would be here. Gamma Wing would have been encircled and overwhelmed. You would never have existed. Don't look so enthused, you degenerate! You're mine now. You will exist until I order you to cease."

My hands were clenched in excitement. I'd lost myself in Tsuros' tale. Visions of capital ships going off like a string of fireworks danced before my eyes.

"Now, imagine the chaos manifest that was the Battle of Arcturus! A planet in flames beneath us, the stars glittering with death. Before us, a collaborator fleet, swelling with reinforcements. Behind us, the headless serpent of Strike Force San. Ten to one, Traitor! Ten to one, and we set upon them!

"Again and again, they tried to swallow us, but we stuck in their throats until they choked! We were not alone. A few true patriots remained in Strike Force San. One carrier and one battleship swore allegiance to Chinci and turned their guns on the Reconciler filth in their ranks.

"Three days of battle, Traitor! Three days of go-pills and sorties. Casualties, calamities, carnage! We had to become animals. Every second of life had to be clawed from the flesh of our enemies while they strove to return the favor. But we were better than them, almost ten times better.

"Almost..."

Tsuros trailed away, gazing into the distance. His expression dragged me back into the dismal classroom. For a moment we had both forgotten we were losing the war.

"By the third day, Strike Force San was no more. As its sole remaining battleship tried to flee the system, the hyper-launcher spent its very last torpedo to blow the coward to bits. Collaborator reinforcements kept arriving. There seemed to be no end to them. They couldn't outfight us, but it was increasingly clear they could outlast us.

"Gamma Wing was depleted. Three of our frigates had been destroyed, two had exhausted their magazines. We were down to one Zhanwu with only a third of her fighters remaining and most of her pilots too fatigued to fly. Our sole remaining battleship had only half of her cannon online. Only *Bulldog* was still fully operational. The Ultra-Dreadnaught had been designed for the lengthy battles of the VTS era. She was still in fighting condition.

"At *Bulldog's* helm, Tong Lang Chinci had been awake for the entire battle. Her voice was a tortured rasp, but the orders never slowed. Her eyes were bloodshot, but they never lost their fire. One defender remained, an ancient N'Graya Owlmoon class Ark that could do little more than absorb fire meant for the *Titan Forge*. *Bulldog* flew in close and opened up with her Hypercane cannons."

My head perked back up at the mention. The Hypercane was an iconic weapon that had defined its era, like the katana or the M1 Garand. Tsuros seized on the chance to draw me back in.

"The VTS didn't fuck around, Traitor! Every single thing they did was overkill. When those Hypercanes roared, every microbe on *Bulldog* felt it. Twenty-three thousand explosive bolts per second! Every third bolt was incendiary plasma. When you hit a ship it looked like you were drawing a bead with an arc welder. We quartered that poor Owlmoon, easy as slicing an orange. Remember oranges?"

I nodded eagerly. I would kill for one.

"At last, Chinci had a clear shot at her quarry. *Bulldog* sank her teeth into the last lune and ripped it to shreds. The *Titan Forge* was ours at last, stranded in space! But we'd hooked Santiago's marlin.

"Our artillery was spent, and we had nothing left that could destroy the beast. Alpha Wing was still a week away. Hezo reinforcements were inbound, but we didn't know if they would aid us or attack us. We should have retreated, but we couldn't bear to. Not after all we'd spent.

"Then the Glömer arrived, and it was too late."

The stack of transparencies had dwindled to just two remaining. First the AGA/LAG 81 diagram that had started this whole mess. Then the final sheet, an illustration of three spherical carriers patterned like footballs.

"Here they are, Traitor. Look at them! Those are Goldberg polyhedrae. The Forge technology adapted into carriers. Each of those pentagons is a propulsive-shielding device, the hexagons are fighter bays. The Glömer were only a third the size of one of our Zhanwu, but they were a thousand times more massive. Imagine the power it cost to propel them!

"The Glömer took up a defensive orbit around the *Forge*, like three electrons of a gargantuan lithium atom. It began to move again, the Glömer were towing *Forge*! They didn't even bother attacking us. They expected us to accept we'd been eclipsed.

"We could not. We attacked with everything we had left. AGA/LAG 81s swarmed from fighter bays, wasps boiling from their hives. The 81s were incredible interceptors. They made our A88 fighters look like biplanes. They shot down everything we threw at them, we couldn't get a single missile through.

"During our entire impotent attack, more 81s pullulated from the Glömer. Finally, they hit a critical mass. A horde switched roles and went on the offensive. Harriers! They nipped and nibbled and gnawed us down to nothing. The Zhanwu went down before she could get half of her fighters out. Soon, the battleship shared her fate.

"Admiral Tong Lang Chinci's last act was to overcharge all of her reactors and order all hands to abandon ship. The lifeboats fired off like a cloud of lice lifting from a corpse. I was one of those lice, Traitor.

"I watched the Admiral fly right at the *Titan Forge* with 81s attacking her from every direction. Firing all her guns at once, roaring defiance! The fighters couldn't stop her. She rammed right into the silver skin of the *Titan Forge!*"

I was riveted, scarcely breathing.

Tsuros shook his head.

"It was all for naught. The *Titan Forge* swallowed *Bulldog* whole. There was no massive explosion, no surprise victory. The *Forge* escaped, and we lost.

"We lost, traitor. We've been losing ever since. After the disaster at Da Jiao, a vast purge began. We strung the Reconcilers up in the streets. We raced to discover the secrets of Forge technology, to build new fleets that could destroy the Collaborators. We seized control of High Command and went into full wartime production."

Tsuros gestured at the walls of the prison and let his hand drop.

"We were too late. Now, here we are, Traitor. One last shot to save mankind. One final mission, and you're the one. Do you understand me? The others are just fodder. Never forget that. *You're the one.* Now get the fuck out of my sight."

Tsuros turned off the projector. I scurried away and left him in darkness.

本以高难饱，徒劳恨费声。
五更疏欲断，一树碧无情。
薄宦梗犹汛，故园芜已平。
烦君最相警，我亦举家清。

9
THE GARBAGE LANCE

I paid a terrible price to hear the Legend of Arcturus. I was alone in the barracks that night. Corrupt was comatose in the infirmary, the other inmates were stewing in the waste reclamation tanks. Since the day the others arrived, I'd dreamed of regaining my solitude. Now that it had been forced on me, I hated it.

You're the one.

I woke up rigid from a dream of mulang Chinci looming over my bunk, wearing only the top half of her uniform. She flashed a fanged grin and commanded me to satisfy her. For days afterward, I struggled to keep that image from rising up at the worst possible moments.

Tsuros' story had captured my imagination. I couldn't stop daydreaming about Steel Wave carving its way through the stars. If only I could have flown with them! I fantasized my scrubber brush was a T-GZK burst, scouring collaborator scum off Ursurus instead of mildew off the shower drain.

Just as I finished cleaning the entire barracks myself, the others arrived. They were all filthy and furious, the smell lingered for days. No one would look at me. They hated me now. I wasn't the one who made them spend all night in the sewage tank.

It didn't matter. Everything was part of Tsuros' master plan. In a way, I found that reassuring. He wouldn't put in all this effort if he didn't think we could win somehow. I tried to believe again.

Before, I had been careful not to do too well at flight training. The nail that stands out gets hammered down. Once I stopped caring, I smoked them all. I was completing runs twice as fast as Pirate. The others weren't even close.

It left me with plenty of time to think. I would drift in space, grinding my toes against the footwell as I watched the Murderess and Glutton flounder through the buoy rings. I liked to imagine I was at the helm of *Despicable,* warming up my cannons to put these mutinous dogs out of their misery.

I'm sure they felt the same way about me. The harder I worked, the worse they looked. If we had another purge, I might be the death of them.

Conversations stopped when I drew near. The others were planning something, their eyes were always on me. Finally, the tension got to me. I spent a whole night awake, clutching the lock-knocker under my thin blanket. But none of them had the stones to strangle me.

Another disappointment.

Instead, they started ignoring our labor rotations, sticking me with the worst jobs. I kept my mouth shut and my head down. Any display of weakness would make it worse. The crooked rotation was bound to bite them in the ass.

It didn't take long, just a few days. During morning assignment, Murderess marched up to me with the *Bayonetta de Basura* shouldered like a rifle. This was a two-meter hooked steel pole we used to clean the compactor gears of the refuse chutes. I suppressed the urge to groan.

RC duty was a filthy, dangerous job. The automatic mechanism that used to purge the refuge chutes had been deemed a security risk and disabled. So now, anytime a chute went down, a pair of us had to get in there with the *Bayonetta* while the gears ran. One slip meant getting chewed up and spat into space.

"You're on chutes today, Tsuros' Pet," Murderess said.

"With who?" I asked. It was a two-man job.

"You're on chutes today," Murderess repeated with a grin.

I took the pole from her, wondering how long that smile would last after I impaled her. I looked at the other inmates, wondering if any would speak up for me. This was beyond unfair, it was stupid. It had to be her idea. Pirate's lower lip quivered, but he remained mute.

So be it. I shouldered the garbage lance and headed for the chutes. When I got the hatch open, I stared into the crusty teeth of the gear-maw and despaired. Even with two people, this was the absolute worst duty. I wasn't strong enough. I could barely get the chute open on my own.

I felt the urge to slump against the wall and sob, but if a drill caught me, they would really give me something to cry about. I took a series of deep breaths to try and calm down and regretted it immediately. The chute was ripe.

If there was one consolation, it was knowing Murderess had fucked herself. I could twiddle my thumbs all day and roll on her when the drills came to ask why the chutes weren't working. There was a one hundred percent certainty I'd take a beating and a twenty-five percent chance the drill would feed me into the chute immediately afterward. But whatever happened, Murderess would share my fate.

It was a suboptimal play. I could snitch directly to Tsuros, but then I really would be Tsuros' Pet. I could never win the other inmates back if I went that route. I would become a permanent pariah.

Maybe it was wishful thinking, but I suspected most of the other inmates didn't actually hate me. They hated themselves for fucking up, and I was a convenient proxy. If I snitched, that would change. As I considered it, I realized Tsuros wouldn't even help me. Weakness disgusted him. He'd probably end me himself. I didn't want to go out that way.

There was nothing left to do but figure out a way to clean the chute on my own. I tried to visualize how all the gears and armatures inside worked, how they would react when

I cleared the jam. When I'd done this with a partner, one hooked the jam, the other helped yank them back. I needed to figure out how I could do that alone without getting sucked into the gears.

It took a whole morning of fiddling, propping up the hatch with a mop, and wedging the sealing ring with the lock-knocker. Then I had to crawl halfway into the chute, tethering myself with an extension cord shibari'd into a makeshift harness. When I tried breaking up the jam, the gears freed up suddenly and almost ripped the garbage lance out of my hands. It took all my strength to hang on, and I nearly dislocated my shoulders.

When I climbed out of the chute, I had to hug my knees and weep for real. If I'd lost my grip and let the *Bayonetta* get ripped into space, I might as well have hopped in after it. Losing a tool meant getting skulled.

One by one, I worked the other compactor heads free. I took my time with the other chutes, slowly chipping at the jams until every muscle fiber in my body screamed. It was better to be sore than spat into space.

At the end of the day, I dragged myself to the showers, scuffed to hell and covered in a second skin of grease and gunk. The squadron was already there, sporting a fresh crop of bruises. There was a purple-green starburst hematoma on Murderess' right tit that caught my eye. That had to be Tsuros' handiwork. I had to grin. I knew this would happen.

"What the fuck are you smiling about?" Murderess hissed.

"Hop on and find out," I said, grabbing my crotch.

For a second, it looked like she might try and tear my eyes out, but Pirate guffawed so loud it startled us both. His laugh was contagious, soon the whole flight was laughing at Murderess. The moment passed. I was too filthy to fight anyway.

Corrupt returned from medical that night, a little glassy-eyed but as annoying as ever. The next morning Murderess' reign was over. Corrupt put us back on the normal rotation and no one argued. They needed me.

After flight training, the squadron was ordered to clean the entire ship bay. While the others swept and mopped, Pirate and I climbed into the gantry to clean up a winch battery that had exploded. We were supposed to swap it for a spare, but there were none left in the supply room. The drill who'd let us in only shrugged when I asked where we could find another. Most of the shelves were bare.

Thirty meters in the air, Pirate and I wore rags over our mouths. We cleaned the corrosive residue with plastic scrapers.

"What happened to you yesterday?" I asked, my voice low. We would pull our heads back, suck in a deep breath, then scrape for a bit before coming up for air. I got the story out of Pirate one huff and puff at a time.

"We were on our way here to sweep the bay. Rehnquist and Nordall ambushed us in the corridor and press-ganged us into cleaning the projector room. Rehnquist had a black eye. Even the drills aren't safe from Tsuros now."

I knew at once what had happened.

"I bet you missed the rust on the ceiling bolts," I guessed. Pirate's eyebrows shot up in surprise.

"*Shit!* That was Glutton's fuck-up. What a beating. Wish you'd been there. To catch the error, I mean. Not to share the beat."

Pirate took a deep breath and went back in, chipping at a clump of gel that had partially crystalized. Sparks flew off it. I could smell the ozone through my mask. Pirate pulled away, and I took a deep breath to take my turn.

"It was that OB's stupid idea to put you on chutes. I argued against it, but no one would listen. They all think I'm a fool." Pirate sighed.

I nodded as I worked the scraper.

"I bet she's next," I huffed. Now that her star had fallen, I was sure Murderess would do something crazy and get herself locked.

Pirate paused, then shook his head.

"I think it's Glutton."

"You wanna bet a meal on that?" I ventured. Glutton's times were trash, but Murderess was more volatile than the gunk we scraped.

"Easy money," Pirate said. Under his mask was a grin.

岧峣太华俯咸京
天外三峰削不成
武帝祠前云欲散
仙人掌上雨初晴
河山北枕秦关险
驿树西连汉時平
借问路傍名利客
无如此处学长生

10
THE INTERROGATION

The drills marched me into a tiny room and thrust me into a metal chair bolted to the floor. The debriefing room sat on top of one of the main reactor conduits. The air was uncomfortably warm and probably irradiated. Nordall wrenched my arms behind my back and handcuffed me to the chair. This was it.

I pretended to be exhausted, but inside, I was a pulsar. I vacillated between neurotic dread and lurid excitement. I was about to be executed, but they must have decided to torture me first.

The drills cut the lights and left me alone in absolute darkness for what felt like hours. I became intimately familiar with the heartbeat of the reactor underfoot. Four cycles ran each minute, each lower than the last. The fourth note was too deep to hear, but I could feel it in the soles of my feet.

How would they do it?

Would they beat me to a pulp? Starve me for days? Brand me with a soldering iron? The scenarios in my head grew more elaborate by the minute. I was so aroused, I expected to hear the button of my fly pop off and zing across the cell. What can I say? That's how I'm wired. I didn't choose to be this way.

The door flung wide, and I was blinded by the light. It terrified me. I thrashed against the shackles until I heard boots in the corridor. The gait was as regular as a watch. I recognized it instantly. I froze up, it felt like the air had been sucked out of my lungs.

TSUROS.

"What is your name?" Sergeant Tsuros demanded. I squinted into the corridor. Everything was a glaring blur.

"Traitor! Reporting as ordered, sir!"

"Where were you last night at 0200 hours?"

"Asleep in my bunk, sir!"

His voice grew closer, but my eyes refused to clear. I couldn't rub them, I was shackled to the chair.

"Did you hear anything in the night? Anyone moving around in the barracks or in the hallway?"

"No, sir!"

"Why is that?"

"Sir?" I asked, stupidly.

Tsuros hit me in my right temple with a closed fist. The blow rang in my skull like a slamming door. Glorious!

Suddenly, I could see again. My veins were hot with adulation, my lungs full of air. I was alive.

In that moment, I had the audacity to stare right into Tsuros' eyes without servility or guile. I wanted him to hit me again.

Harder, I wished.

Instead, his clenched jaw melted into a grimace of disgust. A sigh hissed out of his flared nostrils. Tsuros had forgotten I was like that. I wondered how he'd ever gotten to be a drill with such an expressive face. Maybe it was only because I'd known him so long. Maybe I was only imagining it.

He didn't hit me again and pretended not to notice my erection.

"I asked you why you didn't hear anything, inmate."

"Sir! I was asleep, sir!" I repeated.

"The other inmates were more forthcoming with me. They all heard something." Tsuros dropped his voice, leading me down a path. He wanted me to wonder if one of them had said something about me. That was why they left me in the dark for so long. I was supposed to be wondering if anyone had talked instead of edging.

"Sir! I didn't hear shit, sir!"

I was trying to goad him by cursing. Tsuros would have laid out any other inmate, but he ignored the bait.

"You heard nothing unusual?"

"Nothing, sir! I sleep like the dead, sir!"

"Take some time and think about it. I'm sure you'll remember something."

"Aye-aye, sir!"

I spent the next twenty-four hours shackled to that chair, stewing in a pool of urine. Every few hours, a pair of drills would barge in, screaming at me in a flare of blinding light. Rehnquist and Nordall, the dumbest of the drills.

Both men had the same type of face, lumpy and potato-like. Rehnquist's black eye had faded, but I could still tell. I actually felt a little degraded dealing with them, but I liked that, too. I didn't even rate a first-class torturer like Tsuros. I'd been left to the dregs.

Rehnquist said the other inmates had all informed on me. He warned I would be executed if I didn't spill everything. He made some threatening gestures but never followed through. Tsuros must have warned them not to beat me.

Nordall was the carrot. He promised me a drink of water if I would only recite what had happened that night, telling him every detail. I must have repeated myself twenty times.

The showers had run out of hot water after flight training. Chow was a bland gruel of too-green ersatz peas and stringy clots of fab-protein.

Before lights-out, Pirate told us for the hundredth time how he'd outwitted a Hezo ambush at Altair. For the hundredth time, the rest of the squadron scoffed and told him it was bullshit. I crawled into my bunk, laid my head on the thin and unsatisfactory pillow, and that was it.

"Not good enough," Nordall said. He grinned those wide, idiot lips and quaffed the whole glass. I wanted that water so badly. But I *knew*. Even if I told him everything, he would just throw it in my face. I'd only get a few drops licked off the tip of my nose.

As the torture wore on, those few drops seemed more and more worth it. But that was just a small part of me. The larger part was disconnected, exulting in the scene as if I was standing right next to the drills, torturing myself. I was beginning to hallucinate, and I welcomed it. I'd been having terrible cramps for hours. My eyes felt abraded.

"Let's go over it again," Rehnquist suggested.

"Sure thing, sir," I croaked. My voice sounded like I'd been snorting sand.

"He's too weak. Better let him stew here," Nordall butted in. "Do you want that, inmate? How about another twenty-four hours in the dark?"

"Aye-aye, sir."

They turned to leave me there, but I could sense they weren't finished. I counted the steps towards the door: one, two, three. On the third, Nordall swiveled on his heel. His brow was furrowed with what passed for a thought.

"Hey, inmate?"

"Yes, sir?"

"How come you never asked us what we're grilling you for?"

"Sir! You'd tell me if I needed to know, sir."

"You know exactly what happened."

"Sir! I was asleep, sir!"

"Idiot," Nordall hissed. The door slammed, and there was darkness.

For a while, I wondered if they had left Rehnquist behind to fuck with me in the dark. I strained my ears against the darkness, though I couldn't hear anything but the thrum of the reactor. I think I just hadn't noticed him slip out. For hours, every inch of my skin crawled, anticipating his touch.

I had lost all sense of time. I wondered if the others were doing the same, trying to guess at which point each had broken. I was certain I could hold out the longest. As the hours bled out in total darkness, my thoughts flew far afield. I hallucinated that I was Tong Lang Chinci, bloody-eyed on the bridge of *Bulldog,* preparing for my final tilt at *Titan Forge.*

Then I became convinced I was Murderess. I raved at the empty interrogation room, begging the drills not to kill my unborn child. After that, I started to think I had already been executed, and I'd been in Diyu all along.

At last, the clarion of judgment sounded. An angel burst before me in a wreath of transcendent flame.

"Lydia..." I whispered. She'd come back for me at last.

It was just Tsuros, backlit by the corridor. The horns of revelation were only Reveille. The interrogation had gone on for forty-eight hours straight. Tsuros turned on the room lights. I tried to scream, but I could only produce a rasping croak.

Tsuros was clean-shaven. His uniform was perfect, boots shined, and buttons gleamed. But there was a shadow behind his eyes. He wasn't happy.

"Enough games. Last chance before I lock the door and give you another twenty-four without water. I don't care if you die. Do you understand?"

It took all my strength to nod. I wouldn't make it another twenty-four hours.

"Good. Now, tell me, where is it?" Tsuros demanded.

"Whhh..." I strained. The word was like a hot stone in my throat. I hadn't had a drink in so long. I would have lapped the piss off my chair like a dog if there was any way to reach it.

Tsuros brought his ear to my mouth, like he wanted to hear my last words. At this point, they might be.

"Where's what?" I managed.

I got my wish. Tsuros hit me so hard I didn't wake up for three days.

昔日戏言身后事
今朝都到眼前来
衣裳已施行看尽
针线犹存未忍开
尚想旧情怜婢仆
也曾因梦送钱财
诚知此恨人人有
贫贱夫妻百事哀

11
PIRATE'S GALLERY

"PSSST!"

I listened to the whisper in the dim red light, making up my mind what to do about this new development. Through half-lidded eyes, I watched Pirate creep up to my bunk to see if I was awake.

I was always awake.

I'd lied to the drills when I told them I was dead to the world at night. I barely slept at all. When I did, it was very light, a twitch between dreaming and waking. Pirate and I were the night owls of the squadron, the others usually slept like stones. It had been a week since I'd been discharged from the infirmary. We were all back in our routine.

I had expected at least one of us to be executed, but no one was. Instead, Rehnquist lost his buddy. Nordall took the fall, that was all. The others still had no idea why we'd been questioned.

I learned I was the only one the drills interrogated for more than a few hours. The rest had rolled almost immediately. They thought I was brave for holding out, but really, I just liked to be hurt.

Ahem.

For months, I'd watched Pirate fidget in the dim red glow of lights-out, wondering just what the hell he was doing. Were those tiny movements of his shoulder blades some kind of tantric masturbation? Was he twiddling his thumbs? Sobbing to himself? Whatever it was went on for hours, the motions too intent to be mistaken for sleep. Tonight was different. He had been lying awake, tossing and turning. Waiting for me.

"You wanna see something?" Pirate offered, his voice a hair-thin whisper.

It would have been wiser to refuse. While I'd never really subscribed to the official party line homosexuals were an abomination, I was pretty sure I wasn't one.

But I had been in prison for a long, long time. Every night, I stared into the red-tinged darkness, hoping morning would never come. Whatever Pirate intended would be a break in my listless melancholy. I decided I would see what he had to show me.

Luckily, it wasn't his penis. Pirate led me into the latrine. In his hand, he held the short-handled mop we used to clean behind the radiators. My muscles were tense, ready to go down fighting. But instead, he sprang onto the toilet lid with surprising grace.

I nearly panicked as he worked the screws off the latrine vent. Had he found my stash? Instead, Pirate angled in the left-hand side of the vent with the short-handled mop. I had always used the right-hand side.

From his movements, I could tell he'd done this many times before. He retrieved something from deep inside the duct and brought it over to the sink counter.

"Shut the door and turn on the light," Pirate said, his voice low. No one ever turned on the lights at night, I wondered if it would rouse the others. But it was Pirate's show. I flicked on the lights, worried the drills might burst in at any time.

When my eyes adjusted, I looked at Pirate, his green eyes were bright with anticipation. Along the edge of the sink, there was a row of three bright blue plastic dominos. Each was arranged so it sat in its own pool of light from the overheads.

They weren't dominos! They were sculptures. Each was about the size of a playing card, around twenty millimeters thick. Pirate had carved friezes into them. They were impossibly intricate.

My breath caught. How had he done this?

"It's thermoplastic. You can handle them, but only the outer edge. Try not to breathe on them," Pirate advised.

Pirate had carved each tiny sculpture with a thick outer border so they didn't deform from handling. In total silence, I lifted each and marveled at them. I held each up to my eye so I could soak in all the glorious detail work. In the dim red glow of lights-out, he'd worked as delicately as a jeweler. The man had to be part cat.

The first sculpture was abstract. The carving began as a stylized flowing curve, then it broke into three streams. One had scales like a fish, the next had sharp musculature like a climber's torso, the last a river of curly, flowing hair that twisted into a braid. The three streams met at the upper edge of the sculpture and morphed into sharp-edged lines, like the faces of crystal.

In the spaces between the three streams, Pirate had carved entirely through the plastic, separating them with emptiness. This was the practice piece where he got a feel for the material. A mere doodle that must have taken months.

Poking out from the edge of the sculpture were his tools, the two missing sewing needles. It felt like a lifetime ago we'd caught hell for them. I wasn't annoyed about it anymore.

The second sculpture was an antique, three-masted sailing ship, tossed on stormy blue plastic seas. It was a perfect reproduction, from jib to driver. The sails appeared to billow, and I could almost hear the howl of the tempest overhead. It filled me with longing for a world I'd never known, for seas long gone.

The third sculpture was the one that got to me. I held it

up to the light for as long as I dared, drinking in every curve. When I set it down, there were tears rolling down my cheeks.

In tiny slivers of stolen time, Pirate had managed to carve a shred of hatch cowling he'd filched from a disused airlock into a miniature *Venus of Urbino*. The original painting was a woman reclining nude on a couch, with her hand between her legs. Her expression was inscrutable and indelible, like *A Bar at the Folies-Bergere* or *Girl with a Pearl Earring*.

I stared at the swell of her stomach, the slight rise of her breasts, the tiny signet ring on the pinky of the hand poised above the great divide.

I was awestruck. Into a scrap of blue plastic no longer than my thumb, Pirate had carved everything I'd wanted but couldn't express. She was everything missing in my life. Another man might have made a joke, but Pirate only nodded at me. He understood.

It meant so much more, knowing what he'd dared to make these. I don't even want to think about what the drills would have done to Pirate if they caught him tearing bits off an airlock seal. The danger hadn't passed. They could barge in at any time, and it would be instant death for both of us.

Too soon, Pirate gathered up his miniature masterpieces. I couldn't find my words, I could only watch him climbing back on the toilet to push his treasures out of reach with the little mop. I cut the light and cracked open the latrine door as he climbed off the bowl.

In a different time, Pirate would have started a movement. His personality was even bigger than his talent. A meta-material Matisse, or perhaps a polymorphic-paint Picasso. Instead, we were inmates, condemned to death. There's no waste like a war. I wanted to gush and tell him what his sculpture meant to me, but I couldn't find the words.

"How?" I managed at last as we stood in the dim light together. If the drills burst in now, we'd claim we were ships passing in the night on the way to the latrine. We'd still be punished but probably not executed.

"I roll the needle between my fingers to get the point hot

enough to carve. Very fine work. I told you, I would have been great," Pirate said with a rueful grin.

No boasting now, with the others asleep in their bunks. There was a vast sadness in his eyes. It was a part of him he only let show in the dead of the night.

"Why did you show me this?" I asked, wondering why he hadn't picked one of the others.

"You always listen to my stories." He shrugged.

I stared back, sensing there was more he wanted to say. He was nervous to continue but, at last, he obliged me.

"While they were interrogating us, the drills turned the barracks upside down. Like they've never done before. It took days to get everything back together. I've been worried they'll come back and look deeper. I can't stand the thought no one but me will ever see my work. A drill would just crush them and throw them in a refuse chute."

I nodded. It was exactly what a drill would do.

"But why me?" I pressed, wondering if he suspected. I had a paranoid flash this was just another setup, that Tsuros had put him up to this.

"You're the only one who didn't flip. The rest of us were back in the barracks within a few hours. We thought you were never coming back. Tsuros?" Pirate asked. He tapped his left temple to mean the deep bruise on the side of my face.

"Tsuros," I confirmed. The man left his mark.

"The rest of us rolled on each other immediately," Pirate said unhappily. "All our little secrets. We were eating shit the whole week you were in infirm. The drills were still unhappy afterward. I don't think they found what they wanted."

"Any idea what it was?" I asked. My mouth had gone dry.

"No clue. Probably one of the drills did something, and they tried to pin it on us."

"Sounds about right," I agreed quickly.

A flicker of uncertainty went through his face, and there was an uncomfortable silence. Pirate glanced back in the direction of the barracks, then nodded his head towards Murderess's bunk.

"I almost showed her my sculptures. So stupid. I'd be dead now if I had."

"Why her?" I asked. Murderess was the absolute last person I would ever confide in.

Pirate shrugged, and then cupped the air in front of his chest with both hands.

"All men are fools," he said, sounding a little wistful. "I thought she might have a thing for artists."

"I don't think she has a thing for anyone but herself," I countered. Pirate stifled a laugh.

"Maybe so. Anyhow, my secret is safe with you, right?" Pirate tried to be casual, but he had really taken a terrible chance here. He was having second thoughts.

I made the little gesture of turning a key in the side of my mouth and throwing it away.

"Thank you," Pirate said, visibly relieved. "You always keep it close. You still haven't told anyone who you betrayed to get that name."

"And I never will," I said.

Pirate shut one of his eyes and tilted his head in invitation. He was dying to know. I shook my head.

"Were you really stationed on Tau?" I changed the subject. Pirate was always happy to talk about himself.

"Initially, yes. Want to know something funny? It actually gave me a lot of practice. Ship repair isn't far from sculpture. Performing an endoscopic bursectomy on a shrapnel-riddled hull lining is about as hard as rendering lace in marble. A thorascopic sympathectomy of a reactor shield membrane is like carving a block of clay, where a single bad stroke will kill everyone on the dock. There's art everywhere if you go looking for it."

I was already interested, but when Pirate talked about working on ships, I hung on his every word.

"What was it really like there?" I whispered.

His expression clouded.

"It's a dangerous story. Drills might kill you if they find out I told you," Pirate warned.

"Twice?"

He shrugged with his bottom lip tight. Pirate couldn't really accept we were condemned. I didn't press the issue. Then a sound made both of us freeze. Somewhere up the corridor, two drills argued with each other.

"Tomorrow," Pirate promised. The two of us slipped silently back to our bunks.

丞相祠堂何处寻
锦官城外柏森森
映阶碧草自春色
隔叶黄鹂空好音
三顾频烦天下计
两朝开济老臣心
出师未捷身先死
长使英雄泪满襟

12
GLUTTON AND ADDICT

I remember when Glutton joined the squadron. None of us could believe our eyes. He was the largest human any of us had ever seen. When the Hezo captured him, he weighed two hundred kilos. Two hundred! I can't even imagine how much wheeling and dealing it took to sustain that mass.

Even more impressive, Glutton had somehow survived his training flight, burying thirty-nine normal-sized people. His skin hung off him in sallow flaps, and his eyes had retreated into dark pits. I tried to be his friend, but he wasn't interested. It hurt my pride, even more so when Addict came along. Addict was supposed to be the last, before Toucher died and we got saddled with Murderess.

Addict and Glutton were thick as thieves at once. They could not have looked more different. Addict was born on Anubis Station. He had spindly limbs with big knobby quarter-gravity joints. Glutton was raised on Gonegone at 1.6G. He was actually big-boned on top of his ridiculous obesity.

Even now, in his deflated state, Glutton still had a kind of cherubic quality to his face. There was a sense he was once the apple of someone's eye. Addict had a face not even a mother could love, and I mean that literally. He was abandoned at birth. He told us his story with an amputee's nonchalance. He smoked that person away long ago.

Addict had been alive less than forty-eight hours when Anubis Station Security found him whimpering in a compost chute. He weighed just 1,500 grams. The woman who gave birth to him was nowhere to be found. Somehow, she'd managed to conceal her unauthorized pregnancy for seven months. She gave birth alone, in a plumbing access shaft.

There were habitat modules ringing the shaft. Ten thousand people surrounded her, but no one heard a peep. After all that fear and suffering, she dumped Addict in a chute and disappeared. They never figured out her identity.

He must have been one ugly baby.

Things didn't improve. Addict's face was cadaverous, lined with pale welts where the Hezo had boiled away his tattoos with lasers. His eyes were too intent. They would linger while he puzzled out what he could extract from you.

Glutton was the same way. The men each had a hunger they couldn't conceal, an overwhelming desire for more than they were allotted. I doubt the two would have become friends if they'd met on the outside. At best, Addict would have traded Glutton his rations for dope precursors.

But here in prison, the pair became inseparable friends. They chattered every instant the drills weren't around. If we split them up to separate tasks, they would pout and do such poor jobs the rest of us would wind up redoing their work. Eventually, we gave up trying to change them, just like every other person in their lives before us.

Addict never stopped talking, and Glutton absorbed every word like a second helping of dinner. They always talked about the same things, getting high and eating. Addict had an endless chronicle of the dirt he'd done to stay high:

intercepted shipments and waylaid couriers, plundered stockpiles, and ginned-up prescriptions.

Glutton had just as many stories of angles he'd worked to get extra food. He could turn a single sandwich ration into a one-man banquet with an afternoon of wheedling. He'd eaten all kinds of things the rest of us could only dream of. Live crawfish, preserved iceworm, real beef, wild fruit.

It hurts to even consider how much disappeared into Glutton's gullet, how much was shot up Addict's arms. If those two somehow managed to escape, I'm certain they would immediately return to gorging and getting high. But there was no danger of that. Their flight scores were terrible. I could only hope they would execute Addict first. I didn't want to lose my wager with Pirate.

We were in the eighth training course now and starting to look more and more like actual pilots. Even Murderess could pull off most of the basic maneuvers. I'd mastered them all, and I wondered why. Why was there so much focus on movement, and none on targeting? It was all preamble, no punchline. They were training us like fighter pilots, but what could a squadron of fighters do against the Collaborators?

The drills kept cranking up the difficulty of the training sessions. They made us race, setting up obstacle courses of glowing beacon rings and comparing our times. Whoever was the slowest didn't eat, and it was always Glutton.

The drills caught Addict sharing his food with Glutton. Both inmates caught a beating that landed them in the infirmary for a week. This meant they were a week behind in training when they recovered. Their times got even worse.

I noticed some circuit times declined after Glutton and Addict returned, especially Liar's. On one run, Liar came in dead last, overshooting a turn I thought he could have easily made. The fool was going to get himself killed. After his day without food, Liar outright asked the rest of us to sandbag. He'd worked out a rotation of tanked runs so no one would miss eating for two days in a row.

"No."

Murderess was the first to refuse. Corrupt declined with a bit more hand-wringing diplomacy. The rest of the squadron turned to me.

"Fuck that," I said.

A week later, we stared at Glutton's face through the thick glass of the airlock porthole. He was too exhausted to weep. I wound up losing that dinner after all.

西山白雪三城戍
南浦清江万里桥
海内风尘诸弟隔
天涯涕泪一身遥
唯将迟暮供多病
未有涓埃答圣朝
跨马出郊时极目
不堪人事日萧条

13
THE RUBY STORM

It had been weeks since Pirate said, "Tomorrow." I suppose he lost his nerve. After the midnight showing of his tiny sculptures, he was on edge for days. No tall tales, no boasting, and he always had one eye on the door as if he expected the drills to burst in and drag him to the airlock at any moment. Eventually, Pirate must have realized I wasn't going to rat him out, but still, he was distant.

I think he could tell I didn't believe in the mission any longer, and he didn't want to be contaminated. The burst of zeal I'd experienced after learning about Arcturus had faded. I'd settled back into comfortable certainty we were all doomed.

Things were changing. Since the interrogation, the drills had shifted on us slowly, just a degree a day. There was never a point where I could speak up and tell the others we were being boiled. The struggle sessions ended, and Pirate's hair grew back thicker than ever. The drills weren't as derisive, and the beatings were less severe. Now, we had to actually screw up to get hit. Imagine my disappointment.

When Glutton was executed, the opinion around the squadron was: "Well, of course! He was a fuckup." As if we were somehow immune. But I knew we would all have our time in the bore. It's funny how adaptable people are. The training was so long and boring it felt normal. If you're in the belly long enough, you forget you're being eaten.

Being aware of their tactics didn't make me immune to them. One day at flight training, everything lined up perfectly for me. I was running the most challenging course, but it didn't feel difficult. I was fully awake, totally alive in the moment. The Yama felt like a part of my body and maneuvering through the rings was effortless. I beat my previous run by almost seven seconds.

As the drills pulled me out of the Yama, I trembled with exuberance. I wanted to raise my fist and cry out in triumph. All eyes were on me. I remembered that day at the arcade, the recruiters lying in wait outside of the champion's pod. From the ship bay door, Tsuros called out to me.

"Traitor!"

I snapped to attention, ready to get belted for who-knows-what.

"Good run," Tsuros gruffed.

He turned on his heel and left the ship bay. Everyone was frozen in astonishment, even the drills. I blushed in front of the whole squadron, naked and dripping compression fluid. For so long, the drills had been crushing us, literally grinding us into the deck with their boots. My whole body tingled with pleasure at the unexpected compliment.

Good run.

The others mocked me incessantly for days afterward, but I could hear jealousy behind their jibes. Tsuros' words echoed in my ears and churned in the pit of my stomach. This was the man who put me in the infirmary for a week with one punch. He'd starved me, tortured me, taken away my name, and condemned me to death. Two words of praise and I was practically on my knees for him. I'm such a worm.

The drills were satisfied we'd been broken, and they were building us back up. Our briefings became sermons about the fall of mankind, our looming extinction, the virtue of sacrifice. I tried hard to believe. It would have been so much simpler. But that part of me was dead and gone. Two weeks after we watched Glutton's execution, Pirate returned to my bunk.

"Pssst."

Once more, we crept into the red light of the latrine.

"You want to know about Tau Ceti? I'll tell you. But fair is fair. You have to tell me how you got your name."

I shook my head and looked away.

"It's not even a good story," I grumbled. It wasn't, and I didn't want to tell it. But I wavered.

"Let me see her again, and I will," I bargained.

Out came the short-handled mop. Pirate climbed back onto the toilet to retrieve his miniature masterpiece from the vent. I spent a few minutes marveling at the tiny Venus until anxiety impinged on my enjoyment. There hadn't been a night inspection in a long time, but the fear was still fresh.

With sadness, I relinquished her. We cut the lights and cracked the door. Pirate had a strange look. He was eager, yet afraid. Once he began the story, it all poured out of him.

"Tau Ceti was a mechanic's nightmare. You couldn't have picked a worse place to fight. A system choked in ruby-red dust, rife with ion storms, debris, and ambushes. I'm lucky I only had to pick up the pieces. I was stationed at the Ahklys Orbital Repair Bay. The workload was soul-crushing: meteoroid strikes, shrapnel from minefields, and even sabotage. We were at twenty-five percent casualties before we even spotted a collaborator ship!

"Worse, the dust and debris didn't seem to bother the Clabs. This was their home. The attack wings we sent to hunt them never returned. Destroyed? Deserted? No one knew. We never found a trace. Morale was awful. High Command had us disable every ship's escape pods. Too many deserters.

"After a year of watching their ships disappear, High

Command decided something had to be done. They brought two fleets to Tau, trying to force the Collaborators to flee, or stand and fight. If they fled, the second fleet waited to annihilate them. If they fought, they were surrounded and vastly outnumbered. But the Clabs didn't do either. They hid in the dust like mites.

"They would pop out to bait us into chasing them, then they'd vanish into the red without a shot. They didn't even need to shoot at us. Our ships came back so chewed up by debris they could barely fly. Those were busy times for me, eighty-hour weeks. If the Hezo had any wits, they would have simply abandoned the system."

"Yet, here we are," I said, gesturing around the red-lit latrine. Pirate nodded.

"High Command was too proud to turn tail, even though we were on the verge of losing the war without fighting a single battle. Finally, they came up with a plan."

Pirate glanced back at the door. He was about to get into the deep water.

"Do you know about the Silt City Datasha?"

I had come across a few references to the massacre, but I shook my head and feigned ignorance. I wanted to see what Pirate knew.

"The plan was to *pacify* Ahklys to lure the Clabs into a fight..." Pirate trailed off. His eyes grew distant.

"What happened there?" I pressed.

Pirate swallowed and shook his head.

"I wasn't there. I didn't see what happened, and the Hezo kept everything quiet. But I could see a change in the ones who went. Atrocities written on their faces. Like Addict's scars."

Both of us glanced back at Addict's bunk through the crack in the door. He had wept himself into an uneasy sleep. His face was furrowed in the crimson light, lost in some nightmare.

"How many?" I asked.

Pirate just shook his head.

"It must have been bad," I ventured. I knew it was. Calling the Datasha at Silt City *bad* was like calling UY Scuti *big*. But I had to pretend I didn't know. There was a long silence, and I remembered a legend from Old Earth.

天生萬物以養人
人無一善以報天
殺殺殺殺殺殺殺

I recited, counting the seven kills on my fingers so I didn't lose track.

"I haven't heard Polexian in a long, long time. What does that mean?" Pirate asked.

"Can you understand any of it?" I was still testing him.

"Something about gods that died of starvation? Then it's just death, over and over."

At last, I knew Pirate was really a Polomen. Polexian is as far removed from Middle Mandarin as the Archaic Chinese on the Shang oracle bones. But traces linger.

"It's Mandarin," I told Pirate. His eyebrows raised.

"*Heaven brings forth innumerable things to nurture man. Man has nothing good with which to recompense Heaven. Kill. Kill. Kill. Kill. Kill. Kill. Kill,*" I translated.

"Is that Mao?" Pirate guessed.

"Close, but no. The author's name was Yellow Tiger. He led a bloody peasant revolt. He had that poem inscribed on a monument to murder called The Seven Kill Stele. They said he would cut off the feet of women and burn them in great piles he called heavenly candles. It's probably all exaggerated. Nothing from that era can be trusted."

"What's changed?" Pirate joked.

Instead of laughing, I searched his eyes. Was he starting to crack? What if he lost his faith? Until now, the thought of escape had been impossible. But Pirate had done it before. With the drills weakening, did we have a chance?

"What happened after the Datasha?" I asked, not letting myself get too carried away. Pirate could still roll on me.

"Lancers," Pirate whispered. "Collaborator artillery ships. At the time, most Hezo space weaponry was missile-based. They set up their defenses and countermeasures assuming they would face similar opponents. Effective in open space, but worthless in a system-wide debris disc. We weren't worried about it because the Clabs weren't shooting back. But everything changed after the Datasha. It was like popping a hull-worm cyst."

I grimaced. It was one of those experiences no one ever forgot. That rotten smell, the little shrieking sound they make, the white lines writhing off in every direction. Pirate watched me closely, testing me like I'd tested him. Only someone who'd worked on ships would have that reaction. I gave him a quick nod of acceptance. There was no use trying to hide it.

"I figured. Good, I can be technical. The lancers were mass-drivers, like nothing we'd ever seen before. Eight KT slugs at three thousand kips."

I sucked in air through my teeth as I calculated. Throwing that much mass required enough juice to power a small moon for a year. It meant the Collaborators had discovered something groundbreaking, an entirely new kind of reactor or one hell of a battery. It tracked with Tsuros' story of the *Titan Forge*.

"That's a hell of a shot," I ventured.

"All of our interceptors were worthless. Point defense arrays, chaff, flares, nothing worked. You can't shoot something like that down. We couldn't retaliate. The Clabs were nowhere near us. Some of the shots came from a million kilometers away. Direct hits on reactors through a million clicks of dust and debris. What can do that?"

"Tai Di," I whispered. My hand shot to cover my mouth afterward. I couldn't help it. The aversion to the name had been beaten into me deep. Pirate blanched, and we both shot our eyes back to the barracks door. I felt like the drills would kick down the door and execute me for breaking the taboo.

"We called it Big Two in those days," Pirate said, smoothing over the gaffe.

"I thought it couldn't kill people?" I said. I'd never heard of Tai Di attacking people directly. If it could, why were any of us still alive? The entire Hezo should have been eradicated.

"Here's my guess. The slaughter at Silt City hit some threshold where Tai Di was willing to intervene. It lined up the shots, then maybe it needed a human to actually pull the trigger. *Dim Mak!* The Hezo spent generations building those fleets. The Zhanwu carriers had crews of ten thousand. A single shot and *boom!* Instant death."

"How many?" I asked, trying to imagine it.

"Forty! Forty capital ships in less than a day. They lost a dozen more on the retreat, everything in chaos. The command ships were the first to die. Once the big boys ran, the wolves came out. The Clabs hunted down everything that flew, from scouts to supply ships. The call came down to evacuate the ORB. On the way out, I caught a glimpse of the night side of Ahklys."

Pirate swallowed hard, his jaw tight with anger.

"It was dark! The whole fucking planet was dark!"

"Maybe they were blacked out against bombardment," I suggested. I was afraid Pirate was about to start screaming. But he bit it down, furiously shaking his head.

"Two billion people lived on Ahklys," Pirate hissed. "That was the day I made up my mind."

"To desert?"

Pirate nodded. His eyes glittered in the red light.

"But I couldn't get away. I'd been too proud of my skills, I showed them too much. The leash was tight in all the chaos that followed. I'd been a prisoner all along, you see. They just didn't call me one. I kept getting shuffled to new posts, then there'd be another coup, and they'd send me somewhere else. After the Severance, I was reassigned to a prototype vessel, *The Ganglion.* It was a kind of stealth mobile shipyard, meant to hide in comet trails and orbital rings, slowly assembling an armada. Very *mi.*"

I nodded, it sounded like exactly the kind of harebrained Wunderwaffe the Hezo would fund.

"We didn't just lose ships at Tau Ceti. It was a turning point in the Cipher War. There were many deserters and captured ships. After that point, only full-organic ships were considered safe to fly. Like these bombers we're training in, they're all meat except the hull and reactor."

"You think they're bombers?" I asked. I'd been wondering what our mission could be.

"That's what I think. Why else would they be so big?" Pirate reasoned. "The training doesn't make much sense to me. All maneuvering, no targeting? Bombers don't dogfight."

"Maybe the targeting comes later," I guessed. I was glad to hear I wasn't the only one who thought it was strange.

"Maybe. Do you remember the drills used to have radios?"

I managed not to gasp. I nodded carefully.

"They're regressing tech all over. The Clabs are getting closer," Pirate said. "Supplies are spent, no freighters coming. Whatever their *Shengmu* mission is, they'd better get to it. Time's running out."

I nodded, giving Pirate a meaningful look. Had he broken through the brainwashing? Was he open to making a break for it? If I guessed wrong and Pirate rolled on me, I would die.

"Want out?" I whispered.

Pirate shook his head.

"Too old. I don't have that kind of fight in me anymore. Besides, it's impossible—"

There was a sputtering sob from the barracks. I could see Addict's eyes were open. He stared at the ceiling through the slats of the vacant top bunk.

"Tomorrow," I promised Pirate in my lowest whisper.

I walked over to Addict's bunk. He looked up at me without a word. I pointed to my mouth, then to him, then ran my finger across my throat.

You talk, you die.

Addict nodded. I could only pray it would be enough.

岁暮阴阳催短景
天涯霜雪霁寒宵
五更鼓角声悲壮
三峡星河影动摇
野哭千家闻战伐
夷歌数处起渔樵
卧龙跃马终黄土
人事音书漫寂寥

14
BLACKOUT

There were six prisoners left alive. Myself, Murderess, Liar, Corrupt, Addict, and Pirate.

If the others were telling the truth, they'd all started off in a training flight of forty inmates, just like mine. Subtracting the handful who had become gofers or died in legitimate accidents, at least two hundred and fifty prisoners must have been culled by the drills. Sealed naked inside the airlock and blasted on a garbage trajectory, bound for deep space. A string of frozen corpses, sailing into an indifferent infinity until the end of time.

Why us?

I searched the faces of the other survivors, trying to figure out what common quality we shared. Why had the drills chosen us when so many others perished? They couldn't have picked six more different people. Maybe that was the point.

Whatever the drills wanted from us, they would have it soon.

The difficulty curve of our training wasn't linear. At the start of the flight exercises, the beacon rings were wide enough to fly three ships through. Now, they had shrunk to the point where there was barely a meter of clearance for a Yama to fly through. Anything but a bullseye and the ship would clip against the ring. That was an immediate failed run.

Worse, if we struck the ring hard enough, the cockpit would recoil, contracting with crushing force. Murderess blacked out in a high-G turn, her fuselage striking a ring mid-spin. She had to be towed back to the ship bay. When the drills pulled her out, she was sobbing. Her eyes were blood red, and her entire body was one big, ugly bruise. The drills still made her fly the next day.

I hit my share of rings, though never that hard. Every time I felt my ship crushing around me, I remembered Toucher, the inmate who died during acclimation. His voice, high and desperate as he pleaded with the drills. The slaughterhouse reek of the human soup that spilled out when they unsealed his ship.

It's funny. I must have sat through a thousand lectures about the Glory of Mankind and the Destiny of the Hezo. I can't remember a single thing about them. But I will never, ever, forget that smell.

The memory motivated me as the other inmates flamed out. One by one, they hit the absolute limits of their reflexes. They'd have a disastrous run and lurch out of their ships, battered and bloody as cage fighters. They would cling to the dock grating and weep until the drills carried them away. There was no mercy. Not long after the rings were downsized, the drills fitted them with thrusters. After that, we had to fly through moving rings.

I never broke. The others hated me for that, but what could I do? It wasn't my fault they couldn't hack it. Ring 5 was the last colony to surrender to the Hezo. All my relatives died fighting them. I was orphaned and enslaved, living as a human toy in the infamous arcades.

No one who wasn't there would ever believe the depravity I witnessed. Torture, extortion, murder. There were real death matches in those days. People think it's just a legend, but I've seen them.

If I wanted to eat, I had to win. It's a Zen thing. If you lose the moment, you lose. Corrupt and Addict came to me for advice when they started to plateau. I tried to help, but I knew they wouldn't understand. It couldn't be explained. You had to be there.

The gulf widened. Eventually, the drills had to set up one course for the others, then reposition the obstacles into a more challenging configuration for me. Knowing the others were rooting for me to fail made me want to succeed even more.

There were no radios in our ships, of course. We had signal lights, but we didn't dare use them to chat. The drills would have beat us bloody. I had nothing to do while they re-arranged the course but stare at the station and think about how things had changed.

The Hezo didn't build this space station, just as they didn't build their freighters. They're squatters, a pack of apes scratching their heads and *ooking* at the monoliths of the ancients. They can't even keep this place running. They renamed it Awakening House Reeducation Complex. The drills probably have no idea of the history of this place and wouldn't care to learn.

But I knew.

While I was searching for parts in a long-sealed storeroom, I came across an ancient manual. It was written in VTS, but it wasn't ciphered so I could puzzle most of it out. The manual was meant to orient newly-arriving administrators to the station. There was a timeline of ownership.

The VTS were the last empire to hold the station before the Hezo arrived. They had used it to train fighter pilots. Before the VTS, the station was controlled by the Policia N'graya who used the place to churn out augmented super-soldiers. Both the VTS and PNG used the designation TR440 for the station. The original builders were UNESECA. They left no record of why they'd built a secret space station in the heart of a dust cloud.

At the back of the manual, there was a survey of the asteroid the station was carved from. A/XAR2137 used to be a kidney-shaped chunk of nickel-iron, just over five kilometers in diameter. Beneath it was a diagram of the finished station, with the original UNESECA name. I laughed out loud when I read it.

Ananke Station.

From space, the prison looked like a spinning top, carbon black and two kilometers wide. The docking spire was its spindle. The outer rim of the disc was reeded with habitat modules. There was no way to tell which one was our barracks, but I tried to guess anyway.

The entire structure had been blacked out and tessellated with anti-scanner baffling. Outside of a few significant meteoroid impacts, the exterior hadn't changed in centuries. The rot was all inside.

Every day, it got worse. Equipment had been ripped out everywhere, exposed conduits were plugged with epoxy. The automatic locks had been swapped for physical keys. Something about the way the drills jingled as they trudged past the barracks felt absolutely prehistoric.

There were bright yellow pneumatic lines running through the drab halls. Motors had been pulled, many systems now running on compressed air. The military had become Mennonites.

When I first arrived here, Awakening House ran like a clock. Every day was choreographed down to the minute. It was either move in step or be crushed by a stampede. Now, the halls are empty, the drills preoccupied, the schedule hosed.

Sometimes, we waited hours for the drills to show up. There were missed meals and scrubbed sermons. The only constant was flight training. We never missed a session.

Much of the station was offline. Facilities we had used for the entirety of training were closed off. We were led to alternate rooms, sometimes halfway across the station.

As we marched, I spotted slipshod fixes everywhere. Near the ship bay, there was a pool of fluid beneath a badly patched pipe. In the mess hall corridor, a door was wedged open with a "DO NOT CLOSE" sign taped to it. We couldn't turn a corner without running into evidence of incompetence. When something ran out, sweetener, caffeine, indomethacin, that was it. There was never any more.

Freighters used to resupply us at regular intervals. We never saw them, but we could feel the jolt of the linkage with the spindle, the low hum of their massive engines resonating through every surface. None had docked since we began flight training. Maybe the reason the drills were so gung-ho to execute prisoners was they knew they couldn't feed them.

One night, we were all jolted awake by a tremendous *bang*, followed by a roar of depressurization. The red barracks light flickered, the blowers stopped, and the temperature dropped. All I could think was:

Finally.

We trembled in our bunks, blinking as the emergency lights strobed. The squadron was locked inside the barracks. We could only wait for the drills to let us out and lead us to the warmer sections near the reactor. No one came. One by one, the emergency lights faded.

I have never been more afraid in my life. That's the worst way to die, lost in absolute darkness. Each breath felt shorter than the last. I wanted to scream, but I couldn't spare the oxygen. We were finally forced to huddle together for warmth after piling every piece of clothing and bedding in the barracks on top of ourselves.

Pirate was the one who told us what to do. He saved our lives. When the lights finally came on, we were lightheaded from hypoxia.

There was a big shuffling after that. Many of the drills we'd seen every day were gone. Their replacements were disheveled and nervous, uneasy around us.

I wondered if this was my chance to break out. I could kill one of the green drills, use their keys to gain access to the weapons locker, and die in a blaze of glory. But I didn't have the balls. There weren't enough survivors to stage a revolt. I wasn't even sure the squadron would follow me. I didn't trust any of them, not even Pirate.

Somehow, the others saw all this and still believed in the mission. I don't think they were that stupid. I think the others couldn't accept all their suffering was for nothing. The drills provided them with a fantasy that there was a justice, an order in the universe. They cleaved to it with all their might. The other inmates were all so much older than me, but they were still children.

I let them have it. The fantasy was all that kept them together, and I was too tired to swim against the current.

The night after the blackout, I expected Pirate to come to my bunk again. I was ready to tell him my story, eager to pick his brain for what might have caused the explosion. But when he rose, he went to a different bunk.

Murderess.

Pirate and Murderess had been close together in the huddle. The pair disappeared into the latrine. It wasn't to talk. They were quiet, but I could still hear it all. I lay in the red dark, throbbing with envy. The drills must have run out of the suppressants they were putting in our food. I wasn't looking forward to the return of my libido.

This new development meant I didn't have to tell Pirate my story. But I would have rather gotten it over with. Instead, I lay alone in my bunk, turning myself inside-out with want. Pirate and Murderess still hated each other, I could hear it in the way they fucked. Their brush with death had simply flipped a switch, and there was only one way to turn it off.

来是空言去绝踪
月斜楼上五更钟
梦为远别啼难唤
书被催成墨未浓
蜡照半笼金翡翠
麝熏微度绣芙蓉
刘郎已恨蓬山远
更隔蓬山一万重

15
FÜR LYDIA

After a few nights of debauch, Pirate came to my bunk instead of Murderess's. As I followed him to the latrine, I could see her eyes glinting in the dark, serpentine with resentment.

"Will she snitch?" I asked as I shut the door.

"I'll deal with her after this," Pirate shrugged. "Unless you want a go?"

In the crimson light, he couldn't see me turning bright red. Small blessings. I shook my head, and he shrugged.

"A wiser man than I," Pirate joked. "Woman's got a hole in her nothing could ever fill."

"Do you think the blackout was an attack?" I asked, eager to change the topic.

"Not from the Clabs. We'd all be dead. Likewise, we can infer the reactor wasn't the problem since we're still here. It might have been sabotage. But more likely, a meteoroid punched through the hull and hit a distribution node."

"That would mean mag-deflect is down," I groaned. It was a horrifying thought. If the shield was down, it was only a matter of time until we were hit again. "We were stuck here for hours. Why didn't they switch to secondary power?"

"Probably no one left who knows how. We very nearly froze to death," Pirate agreed. "And they're still having issues."

I felt the chill of the void. All those faces I'd seen howling in the airlock came back to me. At every execution, I'd told myself it couldn't happen to me because I was squared away. Now, I might taste space through sheer incompetence.

Life support is quadruple-redundant. I boggled at the sheer number of stupid decisions that must have happened to get us to this point. Had the drills executed every competent engineer on the station?

"We could..." Pirate began to suggest something, but our eyes met, and the words died in his mouth. I knew what he wanted to say, and why he didn't say it. The two of us could probably fix the damaged node, or at the very least reroute it. But there was one thing we both knew for certain, no matter how bad things got.

Never volunteer.

"It was like this on *Ganglion*," Pirate recalled. "There were forty-eight fabricators, but only ten were online, running at half-capacity. Command still expected us to produce at full output. I hated the fabricator repair crew. Those apes couldn't fix breakfast. On top of that, OpSec kept pushing out these security patches that broke half of the functions."

"You never told me how you managed to steal a ship," I reminded Pirate, nudging him toward thoughts of escape.

"Ha! Stole? Impossible. The Hezo isn't *that* stupid. OpSec keys the ship templates so mechanics can't fly them. There would be nothing but empty repair bays if they didn't. I couldn't possibly steal one."

"Then how'd you get out?"

"I really did build one myself," Pirate smiled. "Piece by piece. OpSec never laid a hand on my ship because they didn't know it existed."

It was an extraordinary claim, and anyone else would have scoffed. But I had seen a side of Pirate the others hadn't, a little blue masterpiece hidden away in the latrine vent. I nodded.

"The fabricators were driving me crazy. One night, I stayed behind after hours and cracked the fabricator open.

That was such a risk. I'd never worked on one before, and if anyone caught me, I might have been executed as a saboteur. But I couldn't bear to wait three days for a ten-minute fab anymore. Luckily, it was an easy fix. The next day, our fabricator miraculously starts running at full capacity."

Pirate grinned widely.

"That quarter, my team launched twice as many ships as the other bays. Command wanted to know why. When they started investigating, I was the obvious culprit. No one else had the chops. The head of the fabricator repair team made a big stink and tried to have me executed for tampering with his machine. As you can see, he didn't succeed." Pirate patted his chest.

"They locked him, promoted me, and gave me command of his squad. They were all worthless. Anyone with promise had been sent off to die at Sigma Draconis. I just gave the dopes a bunch of make-work to keep them occupied. I fixed all of the fabricators myself. It was murder but, pretty soon, I had everything running at a hundred percent. I was a hero."

Pirate had a wistful smile, caught in some memory he kept for himself. I didn't press him. When it faded, he resumed his tale.

"But I made a terrible mistake. I fixed everything and put myself in a situation where I had nothing to do. The boredom nearly killed me. Spare time in a prison is slow poison. I had hoped if I could keep my head down and make myself indispensable, maybe I would find an opportunity to escape. But *Ganglion* was locked-down tight. The Hezo was never going to let any of us leave. Too *mimi.*"

Pirate sighed.

"It got to me. I started to think more and more about taking a spacewalk. Just walk up to the lock one day and WHOOSH! No more struggling. I must have walked up to that airlock twenty times. I couldn't do it."

I understood him completely.

"I needed a reason to go on. I found it in bay nine. That bay was empty and mothballed because the fabricator was beyond repair. Sometimes, I would cannibalize it for parts. I soon realized no one else ever went inside. I was the only one with clearance. That's when I got the crazy idea that maybe I could build my own ship."

"Impossible," I breathed.

"Ha!" Pirate cried, and his hand rose to cover his mouth, he'd gotten carried away. "You see, there were so many levels of unnecessary security. There were factions in command, all suspicious of each other, vying for their turn at the wheel. I performed an essential role and never squeaked. My superiors started to see me as part of the machine, and then they forgot I existed. I had nothing but time.

"Each time I serviced a fabricator, I was required to do a test print to make sure the heads were aligned and everything was up to spec. I was supposed to dispose of the test parts, but I didn't. I brought them to bay nine. Bit by bit, I built an entire pinnace. It took five years."

"Five years!" I hissed. "How old are you even?"

"Too old." Pirate grinned.

"Where'd you get the reactor? How'd you mount it?"

Pirate tapped the side of his head.

"Smart kid. That was the hardest part, the last piece of the puzzle. The reactor in the dead fabricator was still good, but it was impossible for me to pull it alone, and someone in ops would notice it going offline. Getting that reactor out of the fabricator and into my ship was a two-man job, it had me stumped for a long time."

Pirate smiled again.

"A funny thing happened. One day, *Ganglion's* rotational guidance array malfunctioned. The whole ship spun down to .1G. It was pandemonium onboard. It just so happened I had a crane lined up and ready to go in bay nine. Even at a tenth of a G, pulling and mounting that reactor nearly killed me. But I did it. The pinnace accepted the reactor, and everything came online. By the time the dolts in Operations had *Ganglion* spun up again, me and my new ship were halfway out of the system. I named her *Guernica*."

Pirate's eyes grew lustrous with the beginnings of tears.

"For a whole week after I escaped, all I could do was laugh. Every time I thought of OpSec looking around that empty bay with stupid looks on their faces. It was glorious! I just sailed and sailed, through empty systems, into the deep black. I didn't need anything or anyone. I was reborn."

The tears came. Pirate wept in the dim red light of the latrine.

"Of course, I was so selfish. I cared only for myself in those days. That's all over now, I understand I have a role to play and a debt to pay," Pirate said, echoing the lines the drills had hammered into us a thousand times. Then he lifted his head as if hearing a distant note.

"But they can never take my voyage away from me. I was a man. I was free."

I set a hand on Pirate's shoulder. I hadn't touched anyone by choice in a long, long time. He nodded, and I retracted my hand, feeling awkward. Something had changed after the blackout. We'd all been on edge, suffering from feelings that were raw and excessive. I wondered if we'd been on mood stabilizers this whole time and the supply had finally ran out.

"Well, now you know how I became Pirate. Why do they call you Traitor?" Pirate asked.

I swallowed, wishing I hadn't made the deal.

"It's stupid. I didn't do anything interesting," I hedged. I wanted so badly to weasel out of telling him, but Pirate would not be denied. He kept staring at me.

"A Lydia," I confessed. That should have explained everything. But Pirate was too old. His eyebrows arched.

"Who's Lydia?"

"A succubus program. They rove the nets, looking for lonely men. When you fall for one, they slowly win you over to the Collaborators."

"A program?" Pirate was dumbfounded.

"It's slow and subtle. On the anonymous nets, they look like any other chatter. They play games with you. You become friends. They find out everything about you, all the things you would never tell anyone. Anytime you're down, they're there.

They're always interested in what you have to say. Lydias care, in a world where no one gives a shit about you. If you're in trouble, they'll lend you money or help you fix things with the police. I knew it was too good to be true. But I couldn't stop. She knew me, every part of me. She accepted me in a way no human could. Nobody ever wanted me like that. Nobody ever loved me. So I flipped and joined the Collaborators."

"For a woman who didn't exist?"

"She exists."

"But you could never— I mean, she has no body, right? You never fucked her?"

I shook my head. I had never fucked anyone.

"I was going to serve my time in the Clabs and get patterned into Tai Di so I could be with her always. But the Hezo conquered Keilu. They severed the nets, and I lost her. I fell into a deep despair. I couldn't eat, couldn't sleep. Finally, I went to a *Zisha*."

"What's that?"

"A suicide merchant. But instead of waking up dead, I was a prisoner. The Hezo had taken the place over and turned it into a trap."

"You betrayed mankind," Pirate said, pulling away from me.

"Yes," I admitted.

For a moment, he seemed on the verge of turning away in disgust. But then, he was captured by a sudden zeal.

"But you changed! You're the best pilot, the hardest worker. You never whine like the others. You must have seen the light!"

"Yes, of course," I blurted. "I'm ashamed of what I did. I can only hope to redeem myself through the mission." I searched his face, scanning for some sign he believed me. Even if I was going to die, I didn't want it to be in an airlock.

Pirate clasped my hand ferociously and clapped me on the shoulder.

"It's always darkest before the dawn, brother. Victory is destiny."

They had him still.

独坐幽篁里
弹琴复长啸
深林人不知
明月来相照

16
LOOSE LIPS

Why did I think Pirate could keep a secret?

I should have lied. I'd concocted a story to tell him. I was going to claim I'd been in SecOps until I screwed up and caused a data breach that got three ships destroyed. Three ships seemed like a small enough number that no one would call bullshit, but large enough it was plausible for me to be condemned.

But I didn't go with the lie. I got all choked up listening to Pirate go on about how he'd been free, how he was a man, all that rot. I wanted to be honest with him.

I was a fool.

After my heart-to-heart with Pirate, Murderess joined him in the latrine. She had a different kind of x-to-y in mind. I could hear them until the early hours of the morning, grunting and giggling. I tossed in my bunk listening, wishing I hadn't refused Pirate's offer. But I didn't have the nerve.

The next morning, Murderess and I were the last two inmates in the flight line. We watched the drills struggle to get Addict into his ship. It had been like this since the blackout.

There used to be enough drills to load-in the whole squadron simultaneously. Now, they had to do it one at a time. The rest of us had to stand there, naked and shivering in the vast bay, as they waited for their turn. I was always last.

The others didn't take very long to load in, except for Addict. It took the drills forever to get his ship to stop flinching for long enough to get him mounted in the cockpit.

Addict's ship had always been finicky, and it had only gotten worse since Glutton's execution. Perhaps the ship could taste his turmoil. I didn't blame the ship. I wouldn't want Addict inside me either. On a bad morning, it might take the drills fifteen minutes to get him hooked up.

Murderess and I stood at attention on the freezing deck while the drills shouted at Addict to relax. They should have just loaded him in last, but I wasn't about to be the idiot who got beaten for pointing that out. Instead, I spent the dead time staring at my ship, racking my brains for some way to escape in it.

Our ships were brand new, gleaming and flawless like nothing else on the station. The Yama Ten Infiltrator. Fully organic, except the reactor and the payload. They were shaped like giant sunflower seeds. The husk was a meter-thick layer of corybantic phase-diamond.

Phase-diamond is photo-absorbent, the top half of the ship a gradient of purple-to-black from the harsh lights of the ship bay. The underbelly was crystal clear. I could see the ship's innards pulsing, coils fed by the deep shadow of the pseudomitochondrian powerplant.

The cockpit was towards the seed's point, the canopy a living lens that linked to our interfaces. There was no instrumentation inside the Yama, only a pair of spur controls and the bulb trigger that armed and deployed the bomb. *Squeeze-twist-tug-push*, the firing sequence burned into my muscle memory forever.

During the later stages of flight training, the squadron was weaned off using air tanks and forced to use the canopy frill. This was a sphincter of ship-flesh that would close around the neck, sealing the head inside the canopy bubble. The frill would flood with oxygenated compression fluid. We'd all had to learn how to breathe liquid. It felt like drowning every time, and our chests would ache all day as the fluid slowly drained out of our sinuses.

On the actual mission, we wouldn't use the canopy frill. The whole cockpit would be flooded with compression fluid, and we'd drift in our space wombs. Respiration-assist would pump against our diaphragms so our lungs didn't succumb to the strain of breathing fluid for months.

Running along the seam of each ship's husk was the field generator, a silvery vorpal edge that could cut through space itself. The ships were thirty meters long, fifteen wide. Pirate was right, they were too big to be fighters. At the same time, the Yama were too small to be effective bombers.

An F-Cascade bomb wouldn't fit in those tiny bays. There was barely enough space for a conventional fusion bomb. That couldn't be the plan. It couldn't be worth all this just to level a mid-sized city.

Whatever the Hezo intended, I couldn't see a way out of it. Many things made the Yama unsuitable for escape. First, I couldn't simply hop in one and turn the key. Loading up for a flight was a careful process of aligning the hood interface with my implants, cathing up, and being exactly situated in the G-harness pocket. A slight misalignment and my ship would crush me into soup.

On a long-term flight, I would have to be in homeostasis. There would be rectal and feeding tubes, a special coating applied to my skin to keep the ship from digesting me. There were a hundred different steps of preparation impossible to do on my own.

Even if I could convince someone to be my conspirator, they too would need someone to load them in, or they'd be stuck on the station to face a terrible reprisal. Which member of the squadron would be willing to die for me? I was certain none of them would.

Even if I could somehow steal my ship, I would be going nowhere. These were low-mass, stealthed ships. The reactors were tiny, minimal-emission units, incapable of independent FTL. Early in training, I assumed we would be deployed via a carrier, but we never trained on carrier launches. As we drew closer to the mission, I became certain there wasn't enough time left for us to learn. That left only one alternative. They were going to shotgun us.

I was so excited when I realized it. A UNESECA ringship! It was the stuff of legends.

There's very little N'Graya or VTS tech still in service. Most of their ships and machines became useless in the early stages of the Cipher War. They were too complex and presented too many vulnerabilities. The Hezo tried to harden some of their more essential machines, but they were bailing water.

As the empire aged, there were fewer and fewer people who understood the ancient technology, and parts grew scarce. Finally, a day came where there was no one left who could fix the machines. We witnessed it every day in the microcosm of our prison.

UNESECA was different. They really thought their empire was going to last for millennia, and they built like it. Their ships were self-sustaining, monolithic, and vast beyond anything the regimes that followed could even attempt. The entire Hezo Collective Prosperity Sphere was built on the backs of stolen UNESECA freighters, and the guns of UNESECA frigates.

As these irreplaceable ships were lost, the empire waned. High Command would give anything to rediscover the secret of their mass-inverter drives. Anything except the freedom scientists would need to actually figure them out.

Ringships are another UNESECA miracle we can't begin to understand, much less replicate. There are only a handful of functioning pairs left in existence. Each is comprised of two gargantuan ring-shaped ships, requiring a crew of fourteen-hundred to operate.

It takes hours of meticulous alignment and hyper-charging batteries to fire a ringship pair. When they function as intended, everything inside the cylinder of space between the two rings is propelled at some ungodly multiple of C. When they fail, it's cataclysmic. If the Hezo was willing to gamble a ringship duo on us, it meant we really were their Shèngmǔ play. We were their last hope.

I had always wanted to see a ringship in person, and I was still excited, though I knew they were harbingers of doom. The ringships would be bristling with elite troops and guarded by frigates. If I wanted out, I needed to come up with a plan before they arrived. I'd never dreamed I would survive long enough to actually fly the mission. Now, time was running out. Escape was imperative.

While all this was coursing through my mind, I felt the subliminal anxiety of being watched. I turned my head slowly so as not to draw the attention of the drills. Fortunately, Addict's ship was still giving them problems.

Murderess stared at me. I shot her a look of reproach. Was she trying to get us both beaten? She faced forward, but as she did, there was a little smirk at the corner of her mouth. *She knew.*

My stomach plunged. Immediately, I realized Pirate must have told Murderess about Lydia. He'd looked queasy all morning. I'd written it off as lack of sleep, but it wasn't. Murderess had wheedled my secret out of him, and now, he was consumed with guilty fear.

For good reason. I held absolute power of life and death over Pirate. Two words to Tsuros and Pirate would spend forever tumbling naked through space. *Latrine vent.* Staring into the void through exploded sockets, his loose lips frozen wide in an eternal scream.

A wicked smile crossed my face. How he would suffer!

I stood at parade rest, my hands tightened into claws behind my back. What about Murderess? I could inform on her as well, but she was right next to me. The drills were a hundred meters away. I wondered if I could strangle her before they could stop me. My vision went red. I could almost feel my hands closing around her neck.

Murderess gave a startled snort, interrupting my fantasy. Her eyes had dropped to my crotch. Her eyebrows rose.

I realized I had become aroused. The shame of having my secret revealed, the thoughts of violence, and her mocking stare had set me off. I couldn't let the drills see me like this! I had to shut my eyes tightly, tensing my thighs until they were stiff as oak.

I sent my mind hurtling along terrible paths, thinking about suffocating in the barracks, mucking out the elevator shaft, and the human soup spilling out of the ship hatch. I was too busy killing my erection to kill Murderess.

By the time they got Addict loaded in, I had a handle on it. As they walked Murderess over to her ship, I glared at her back, practically incandescent with hate. I desperately wanted her to crash into a ring and get crushed into paste.

Instead, I was the one who hit a ring, bewitched by emotion. I had to halt and force myself to breathe the compression sap more slowly. I pushed my rage away so I could complete the course. If I messed up again, the drills would want to know why. I didn't trust myself to stay quiet. I would get us all killed. I finished without another error, but it was my worst time in months.

When they pulled me out of the ship, sputtering and shaking, I noticed the rest of the squad all stared at me.

Everyone knew.

I hated him. I hated her. I hated them all!

风急天高猿啸哀，
渚清沙白鸟飞迴。
无边落木萧萧下，
不尽长江滚滚来。
万里悲秋常作客，
百年多病独登台。
艰难苦恨繁霜鬓，
潦倒新停浊酒杯。

17
THE PHANTOM OF THE VENTS

At the end of every training flight, the drills would unseal our ships and wrench us out of the cockpits, disoriented and sticky with ship fluids. They would hose us off, then blast us dry with compressed air. Today, there was something wrong with the heater. The water was ice cold. Each member of the squadron yelped as the torrent hit them, and when it was my turn, I couldn't help but do the same. The air hose sputtered a feeble raspberry as they tried to dry us. There was a break in the line somewhere.

Losing the war.

I stood shivering on the deck after the terrible run, spirit bruised and manhood shrunken. I could hear the bay doors hiss open behind me, the unmistakable sound of Tsuros' stride. His boots clanged against the deck grating. He stopped in front of me and eyed me up and down.

"Pathetic."

I wasn't sure if he meant my genitals or my flight time. Both were in a sorry state today.

"Come with me," Tsuros ordered. He turned briskly and marched back towards the door.

Before I could comply, a strangled sound escaped Pirate's mouth. The whole squadron flinched. Tsuros came to an abrupt halt, searing us with his glare. Pirate's nose twitched. He tried to pretend he'd been stifling a sneeze.

Tsuros motioned his head towards a drill. Without hesitation, the drill drove his fist into Pirate's gut. Tsuros watched Pirate fall, and then gave a curt nod of approval. I started towards the bay doors, but Tsuros' expression froze me mid-step.

"Get dressed, idiot," Tsuros ordered.

Still wet, I put on my coveralls and followed him out. Pirate softly sobbed behind me.

I expected Tsuros to lead me back to the interrogation room. Instead, he brought me to his office. There were no pictures, no medals, no commendations. Set against the wall was a clavichord. At first, I assumed it must be a replica. An antique would be impossibly expensive. But the open lid had the particular luster of real wood. There was a slight concavity to the keys that spoke of decades of use. It was real. Tsuros was the source of the distant music, the phantom of the vents.

Tsuros, made a sound in his throat, and I snapped my eyes forward, anticipating retribution. He stood behind his desk, where everything was rigidly organized. Each object looked like it had been aligned with a ruler. Maybe they had.

"Rate the competence of your squadmates," Tsuros fired the command at me like a shot, looming over his desk.

I was at attention. He hadn't given me leave to relax.

"Low, sir," I replied. I didn't care about shielding them anymore.

"Their flying ability?" Tsuros pressed.

"Lower, sir."

"Sit down."

I took the chair. It felt like a trap, but I had no choice. My body was damp and uncomfortable. I was going to leave a spot on the chair, and Tsuros might beat me for it, but he'd certainly beat me if I hesitated. I couldn't win.

"You're worthless, but you aren't stupid, Traitor. You can see how things are going."

He gestured around the walls, meaning the prison falling apart all around us. His orderly office was like the eye of a hurricane.

"Say it," he demanded.

I was confused. I hoped I didn't have a concussion.

"Say what, sir?" I asked.

"Say it!"

"We're losing the war, sir," I said. Tsuros was, after all, the one who had unwittingly revealed this to me.

For a moment, Tsuros' lip curled. Maybe he had meant for me to say something else. But his expression leveled.

"That's right. We are losing the war. Losing to an enemy that can't attack us! An enemy fundamentally incapable of doing us harm! And it's almost over, we're nearly finished. All because of people like you. Deserters. Retreaters. Backstabbing, turncoat, *traitors*," he spat the last like a curse.

Had Tsuros brought me here to kill me? The hair on the back of my neck rose. My eyes darted across his desk. I searched for something I could use to defend myself, but nothing would suit.

I had no hope of beating Tsuros in a fight. No amount of adrenaline could overcome our difference in size and strength. I imagined him surging across the desk, closing those thick fingers around my windpipe and squeezing until my face turned purple. Soon, it wasn't just my neck hair rising. I was glad to be sitting down. Thankfully, Tsuros didn't pick up on my inner turmoil. He probably thought I was just afraid.

"The others in your squadron are spineless. Not you. You were a cunt-hair away from dying when we grilled you, did you know that? Forty-eight hours without water. Not a peep of protest. Medical says your kidneys were failing. Did you break into that storeroom, Traitor?"

Tsuros rose to his feet and circled around the small office. It felt like his mouth was just centimeters from my ear. If I flinched, I would get belted for it.

Here was the pivotal moment. It was critical I delay my answer, to act like I was getting new information. I pretended I was trying to figure out who had done it.

"No, sir," I concluded.

"We could shoot for seventy-two hours without water this time," Tsuros threatened. He completed his circuit and made his way back behind his desk.

"Aye-aye, sir" I replied.

I met Tsuros' stare, daring him to do it. Seventy-two hours of interrogation would kill me. I was certain he couldn't afford to lose me. It just bothered him that I hadn't cracked like the others.

Tsuros sat down and faced me, shrugging off the failed attempt. He had more cards to play.

"It's time, Traitor. You fly at 0600."

I was stunned. How could the mission be tomorrow? Whatever the hell they wanted us to do, I knew the others weren't ready. Addict was a mess. Murderess had barely improved. Corrupt and Liar were middling, and who knew what Pirate would do. If this was a tournament, I would expect all of them to get eliminated before semis. I wouldn't trust any of them in a battle.

I wanted to scream all of this at Tsuros, but I choked it down. He didn't really care what I thought. I told myself dying on the mission would be better than dying in this prison.

"Aye-aye, sir," I said, sealing my fate.

"Nothing I say in this room will be repeated. Do you comprehend?"

"Yes, sir."

"Do the others still believe what we've told them about the mission?"

"I think so, sir."

"Do you?"

"No. This is a suicide mission, sir."

Tsuros nodded.

"Are you ready to die, Traitor?"

"Yes, sir," I replied easily. I felt a moment of relief that I'd been right all along. I think I was more worried I'd guessed wrong than afraid of dying. I'd been ready for a long time.

"The broad outline of what you know about the mission is true. But you're correct, there is no plan for retrieval. You'll find out why in the briefing. This is the third time we've attempted this. We sent veteran pilots on the first one. They failed. Then we sent fanatics, the most zealous patriots.

They failed. Now, we're down to convicts. It was the psychologists' idiot idea to send in the condemned, thinking you had nothing to lose. Now, it's too late. The other fronts have collapsed. We're out of supplies, out of men, out of time. You are mankind's last chance."

I stared back at Tsuros, wondering how long he'd spent composing this pitch, how many times he'd rehearsed before my empty chair.

"Look at me, Traitor. I've served the Hezo since the day I was born. I've got more flight hours than every man on this station combined. I crushed rebellions. I conquered star systems!"

Tsuros tapped the ridge of his cheekbone with his index finger.

For the first time, I noticed the very faint scars on his temples. Three pinpoints on either side, forming equilateral triangles where an interface had been removed. Now I knew why he was on the other side of the desk. He'd burned out, and they'd clipped his wings.

Tsuros paused until he was sure I understood.

"The war has turned against us. Procyon is lost. Sirius has capitulated. These cowards want to cede the galaxy to our own creation. Weak, disgusting sheep! Satisfied to graze and rut while our species is extinguished! Wallowing in their knock-off Heaven! Oozing through fat, meaningless degeneration! No contrast! No definition! An easy, useless, painless existence! Do you want that, Traitor?"

My eyes blazed. Tsuros was speaking my language.

"No, sir."

"Your squadmates are weak, Traitor. We should be sending a hundred ships, a hundred first-rate pilots. But there are no more ships. No more munitions. No good men. Just you."

I nodded in agreement.

Tsuros let out a long, dissatisfied breath. When he finished, all emotion had drained from his face.

"The Collaborator fools made a deal with the Devil. The worms are burrowing into the stars themselves, trying to feed the beast. But Iblis can never be sated. They will all be consumed."

My breath caught. Iblis was one of the forbidden names of Tai Di. A year ago, Tsuros would have been executed for saying it, and I for hearing it. But there was no one left to execute us. The Hezo was falling! I was struck by the admission. It took me a moment to process the rest of what he'd said.

"The stars, sir?"

"You'll be briefed before the mission," Tsuros replied, cold and remote. The shifts from fire to ice in his demeanor reminded me of the week after we got our implants.

Cranial trauma.

Tsuros stared at me for a long time. All I could do was peer back. I didn't dare ask why I was here, or if I could go. He would dismiss me when he was finished with me.

"You are the only pilot who matters on this mission. The others are disposable. You are to fly at the rear and let the others take the hits. If they falter, keep going. Get as deep as you can before you trigger."

I couldn't mask my distaste. In my mind, I was always the one at the van in the mission, screaming into the fray.

Tsuros noticed.

"Get that shitty look off your face. Cowering is what you're good at. That's what you are. Why do you think we let you live, *Traitor?* Did you think you were fooling anyone?"

I almost recoiled.

"The psychologists wanted you culled, round one. I said no. They wanted me to keep you in the dark about the mission, like the others. Again, I intervened. This is my show. I know what you are. I know you won't fail me. Now, get out. They're waiting for you in the briefing hall."

I followed his orders. But on the way to the briefing hall, I made a fateful detour.

I know what you are.

Did he really?

诸葛大名垂宇宙
宗臣遗像肃清高
三分割据纡筹策
万古云霄一羽毛
伯仲之间见伊吕
指挥若定失萧曹
运移汉祚终难复
志决身殄军务劳

18
SI HAIDAO

I had an entire year to think about how badly I screwed up my last night on Ananke Station.

It was a long journey to the target. I drifted in and out of consciousness for what might have been minutes or days. There was no light, we had outrun it. Early in the mission, I suffered from hallucinations, phantasmic fractals my mind generated to protest against the darkness unending. But my subconscious grew lazy, and afterward, there was only black.

The ship could sense I was awake and attempted to administer sedatives, but they were increasingly ineffective. Even as a massless aberration, hurtling through a pocket of null-space, I was still an insomniac. There was nothing to do but dwell on my mistakes, drifting in the black diamond of my space-womb.

Every two hundred hours, there was a squadron alignment. Our cockpits would begin to bioluminesce and administer a stimulant, rousing us from slumber. The alarm light shifted from red to green as we woke. When the color shift completed, we had to quickly correct our position and align our ships into the tight jump-ring formation. We flew in a belly-out circle, with our cockpits facing each other. I could see the pale and tiny faces of the other prisoners in the firefly green glow. There was nothing beyond our ships, only the absolute black of null-space.

Our orders were to maintain thirty-three meters from cockpit to cockpit. Some subtle force dragged our ships apart, wrenching us inexorably towards the edge of the null-space bubble. We'd been warned that drifting to the edge meant eternal suffering. At the center of the bubble there was a particle stream that reacted with our canopy lights and became visible. This was the guiding light we used to orient ourselves.

Those brief alignments helped me to keep from going mad in the dark. The sight of human faces was like water in the wasteland. Our canopies were linked to our interfaces. The phase-diamond hull would reshape as we focused, like a second lens of our own eyes.

If I wanted to, I could telescope until I could count Murderess's enlarged pores or Corrupt's individual nose hairs. We all rushed to align our ships as quickly as possible so we could have more time to look at each other.

A few times, I tried signaling to the others using fist-palm code, but none of them knew Morse. Liar and Addict made a few abortive attempts to communicate by drawing letters in the air, but there was so little time to get the message across. Finally, we gave up and stared at each other, amazed at how terrible we all looked.

Murderess was the worst. She was losing weight. I suspected there was something wrong with her ship. Dark patches formed on her skin, while the rest of us had become pale as ghosts. Addict looked like he was in pain all the time.

At first, I thought it was just withdrawal from the LDSM, but he never seemed to get better.

No one had any kind looks for me, and I didn't blame them. We would have only a few minutes to gaze at each other before the ships darkened, casting us into a two-hundred-hour lightless abyss. I longed to see the others now. I could have stared at those four faces for hours. Strange to think I used to hate the sight of them.

I had nothing but time to dwell on it.

When I arrived at the briefing hall the night before the mission, the other inmates were already at attention. Tsuros was waiting for me.

"Where the *fuck* were you?" Tsuros demanded.

"Detour to the latrine, sir!" I said. I wasn't lying.

Tsuros stared at me for sixty seconds. I don't think anyone in the room drew breath for the entire minute. It was the biggest gamble I had ever taken.

"Get your shit together, idiot," Tsuros hissed at last.

The briefing wasn't long. At the end, I could feel the other inmates side-eying me. They all wanted to know if this was some sick joke. I could only stare at Tsuros, my whole being inflamed by the audacity of his plot.

They were bringing in a UNESECA ringship, I'd been right about that. But everything else was beyond my capacity to imagine. The mission was madness.

Tsuros was utterly insane.

Yet, I had to admit, the idea had a certain doomed charm. It was better than anything I could have come up with in his position. Tsuros had created a billion-to-one, bat-out-of-diyu, Hail Shèngmǔ long shot. Literally, the greatest long shot of all time.

His plot whispered to me with the dubious promise of a lottery ticket. What if it paid off? Every day, for as long as I could remember, I had woken up expecting to be executed.

Death had become drab. I had nothing to lose.

I have to confess, in that moment, he truly had me. Tsuros had set my hands at the throat of history. I could feel destiny pulsing beneath my fingers. All I had to do was squeeze.

I was all-in. I regretted my little detour. If the drills found out, they would have to execute me, best pilot or not.

After the briefing, Tsuros dismissed us to early chow. We shambled our way through the halls, trying to wrap our minds around the mission. Each of us mouthed the same idiot denials, shaking our heads.

"A star. A *fucking* star," Pirate muttered. None of us could come up with anything better. The six of us didn't even fill a single table in the empty cavern of the mess hall. There was a single drill assigned to watch us. He was almost asleep on his feet.

The last solid meal of our lives was the same gritty, gray-yellow mash we'd eaten morning and night since the supply ships stopped. But there was a surprise. Each of us was given a single square of blueberry gelatin topped with a dollop of whipped cream.

Dessert!

I stared at it, an astonished, wide-eyed orphan. With a trembling hand, I rocked the little dish, watching the blue cube wobble. I prodded at it with a fork, I sniffed at it. The others did the same. We couldn't believe our luck. I decided I would wait until after I choked down my mash so the taste would stay in my mouth longer.

Of course, Addict couldn't wait. He slipped a spoonful into his mouth, and his eyelids fluttered.

"That's *sweeeet!*" he moaned. Addict rolled the gelatin around in his mouth and smacked his lips with porcine delight. I expected him to get maudlin soon, blubbering about how Glutton would have loved this.

Instead, he sniffed. Addict circled his tongue and sucked his teeth. His eyes narrowed with suspicion. Corrupt had just picked up a spoon when he noticed Addict's peculiar motions. We all waited to see if Addict was about to keel over.

"Pretend to eat. He's looking," Addict said under his breath. I ate a spoonful of the gritty nutrient mash. The others made similar motions. "I think it's LDSM," Addict whispered. "If you want to stay awake tonight, don't eat it."

I'd never tried it, but I knew all about LDSM. Ligdinshymium was popular on Ring 5, among the sort of people who would take cryosleep sedative if no other drugs were available.

"Why would they drug us? They've already carved us up," Liar protested, tapping the hood interface ports at his temples.

"They're putting us to bed, that's all. Doping us to keep us from doing anything stupid tonight," Murderess reasoned. She threw a glance at Pirate.

Pirate was too busy frowning at his gelatin to notice. With a deep sigh, he pushed the tray away.

"Don't let the drill see that," I said in between mouthfuls of mush. "They'll strap you down and inject you if they have to."

Pirate nodded quickly. Of course, they would.

"How do we get rid of it?" Pirate asked. "I don't want to be drugged."

"I do," Addict said. He finished off his gelatin with gusto. "Anyone who doesn't want theirs, I'll take it."

"Will that—" Corrupt began, then he couldn't force the words out. The anti-suicide conditioning was powerful. But Addict shook his head.

"Tolerance," Addict said. He tapped two fingers at the crook of his arm.

"Don't be stupid. He just wants your desserts," Liar protested.

"Eat some then," Addict said. "Just don't be surprised when you black out."

I could already see Addict's pupils expanding. But Liar couldn't trust anyone. He took a bite.

"Tastes like blueberry to me."

"Suit yourself," Addict shrugged.

I was torn. I wanted to eat the dessert. It had been so long since I'd tasted anything that wasn't disgusting. The quivering blue cube promised sweet oblivion. But I'd taken too many chances today. I couldn't risk being unconscious tonight.

I waited until the Drill's eyes drooped towards the floor, then dumped my gelatin onto Addict's plate.

"Enjoy," I whispered.

He did. I had to watch that ugly bastard eat all five of our desserts. Still defiant, Liar finished his own. It took less than five minutes for us to confirm that Addict was right. Liar's eyes rolled, his head lolled, and he could barely finish his mash. Addict watched him with a knowing smile. Even at six times the dose, he was in better shape than Liar. Tolerance was a virtue.

When I got up to bus my tray, I let my head hang forward, affecting a slight zombie shuffle to my gait. The others noticed and took my cue. Liar didn't need to act. He barely made it back to his bunk.

"Lightweight," Addict crooned with an easy smile. That was the only time I ever saw Addict look serene.

Forfeiting our desserts was a mistake. Addict was propped up in his bunk like a fiend in an opium den, grinning at us through heavy-lidded eyes. Liar was totally gone, dead to the world and drooling. We'd been ordered to our bunks and the lights were out. There was nothing to do but wait in the red silence.

Corrupt tried to talk, but our minds were too wet with worry for conversation to catch. Pirate seemed so sad and distant that I regretted what I'd done to him. I hoped he wouldn't find out. Murderess tossed and turned, possessed by some restless energy. I wasn't surprised when I saw her creeping over to Pirate's bunk.

There was a quick exchange, then she returned to her bunk with scornful steps. *Rejected.* Soon after, she rose again. This time she went to Corrupt's bunk. The two slipped into the latrine, and Pirate and I had to listen to every sordid squelch and sigh. It didn't take long. Corrupt slithered back to his bunk, furtive as a schoolboy. He turned his face to the wall.

Murderess emerged from the latrine, disappointment plain on her face. My interest quickened. I expected her to go rub Pirate's nose in what she'd done. But instead, she crept over to my bunk.

"Do you want to try with a real woman?" Murderess offered.

My heart pounded. She reeked of sex, and her voice was sultry. But it was the despair in her face that turned my screws, her wretched need. Corrupt hadn't been enough for her. What did she expect from a bureaucrat? I was more of a man than him. I throbbed with ardent desire to turn the knife in all three of them at once.

But I refused.

"No."

Anger blazed in her eyes. Murderess spun away and stalked over to Pirate, but he hissed something vile at her. For a second, she stood over him with her fists balled and her chest heaving. She looked like she was about to scream. Instead, she went back to her bunk and sobbed into her pillow.

I regretted my decision immediately, but the moment had passed. The four of us languished in the red dark, each desperately unhappy in our own way. Finally, it was Pirate who rose, taking resigned steps towards the latrine.

My revenge was at hand.

Before Pirate even had the screws off the vent, I knew I'd made a mistake. Vengeance was as bitter in my mouth as drugged gelatin. All I could do was lie there in the red, listening to the increasingly desperate sounds of Pirate fishing with the short-handled mop.

An anguished cry rang out in the latrine. He couldn't find his little sculptures. The rest of the squadron tensed. Pirate was too loud. He was going to bring the drills down on top of all of us.

"They're GONE!" Pirate howled.

I had expected him to weep, to get mad, to accuse me, and maybe throw a punch. Not to bellow in the latrine like a madman and get us all killed. But he'd gone insane, Pirate stormed around the barracks, waving his hands at the empty bunks.

"THEY'RE GONE!" he shouted again, flipping over an empty bunk.

I'd broken him.

Boots thundered towards us in the corridor. I had only one option, pretend to be drugged and play dead. Through my closed eyelids, I could see the barrack lights blaze on. At once, two drills barked at Pirate to shut up. But he wouldn't. He raved on and on.

"They're gone! All gone! *Venus, Guernica, Celestine!* All my friends! All my work! My life! IT'S ALL FUCKING GONE!"

I could hear the drills beating him, heavy fists slamming into flesh, but he wouldn't shut up.

"GONE!" he wheezed. One of them must have hit him in the stomach.

"GONE!" The hollow sound of his skull banging against a bunk-post.

"GONE!" Pirate cried once more, and then a sound from the corridor silenced him. Everyone was still, even the drills. Familiar boots were headed our way.

Tsuros.

There was a terrific scramble. I think Pirate tried to get away. One of the drills cried out. I couldn't resist peeking. Pirate had bitten the drill's hand. He was bleeding. In response, the drills kicked Pirate savagely and stomped him into the deck.

"Get off him! What the fuck is going on in here?" Tsuros bellowed. Only Liar didn't wince.

"He bit me, sir!" I recognized the voice, Liu, one of the new drills. His back was to me, but I could tell he cradled his hand. Pirate had taken a chunk out of him.

"Psychotic reaction," the other drill suggested.

"Since when are you a doctor, Ives? Pick this trash off my deck."

Ives hoisted Pirate up by his collar, dangling him so his toes just barely touched the floor.

"Pirate! Are you done crying? Do I need to sing you a bedtime song?"

"You murdered them!" Pirate hissed. "Glutton, Charlatan, Agitator, Drunk Two. You murdered them!"

"Those inmates murdered themselves by fucking up. Do you want to join them? You're hours away from your mission. Don't be an idiot," Tsuros warned.

But Pirate was beyond fear and reason.

"It's all gone! The fleet vanquished! Ahklys snuffed! You're all dead!" Pirate howled.

The foolish words hit Tsuros like a slap. He lunged forward, clasping his hand around Pirate's windpipe. With one arm, he lifted Pirate into the air, cranking down hard. Pirate's eyes bulged, and he clawed at Tsuros, trying to break his grip. But Tsuros' fingers were sunk in like a serpent's fangs.

I watched spellbound as Pirate kicked and writhed and finally went limp. When the dying was through, Tsuros dropped him to the deck with bony *clack* of skull against metal. The barracks filled with the stench of voided bowels.

"This prisoner suffered a psychotic break and began reciting collaborator propaganda. Ives, Dispose of him in lock five. Liu, mop this shit up."

"Sir, my hand," Liu protested. The bite was deep. He leaked blood everywhere.

"Don't you have another hand?"

"Yes, sir."

I shut my eyes and feigned unconsciousness as Tsuros turned towards me. I felt his stare. There was a hunch building at the back of my neck. It took all of my will to keep from shuddering. I battled to keep my breathing steady.

I listened to the sounds of Ives dragging Pirate away. The water ran in the latrine, probably Liu washing out his bite. Then I could hear him awkwardly swabbing the deck. When he exited the barracks, he left the lights on.

Tsuros was still there.

All night, I waited for Tsuros to leave, but he never did. He might have stared at me the whole time, but I didn't dare crack an eye. I was certain his eyes would be centimeters from mine, that the next thing I would feel would be his hands wrapping around my neck. I had to remain motionless for hours. My muscles screamed with tension. Sleep was impossible.

Why did I do it? All he'd done was run his mouth. He was Pirate, what did I expect? I was fool for trusting him and a fiend for shoving his little statues deep into the pipe where he couldn't reach them. For the six most uncomfortable hours of my life, I dwelled on it. One by one, I summoned up feeble excuses.

He shouldn't have told my secret, we were doomed anyway, I couldn't have known he'd go crazy.

I couldn't fool myself. I'd killed Pirate, sure as if I'd strangled him myself. I should have forgiven him. I should have fucked Murderess. I should have eaten that dessert.

"You can stop pretending," Tsuros said at last. His voice was dry as sand. "Time to fly."

群山万壑赴荆门

生长明妃尚有村

一去紫台连朔漠

独留青塚向黄昏

画图省识春风面

环珮空归月下魂

千载琵琶作胡语

分明怨恨曲中论

19
THE FORTY-FOURTH

On the tenth alignment, Addict was in trouble. His canopy frill had errantly deployed. The sphincter was tight around his neck, constricting him like a python. His face was pressed against the canopy, the pressure distorted his features and made his skin livid. Addict's head looked like a sausage about to pop out of its casing.

He tried to catch the eyes of the other pilots. His mouth moved frantically. We couldn't hear him, but he must have been begging for help. Murderess, Liar, and Corrupt all looked away. At last, Addict's eyes locked on mine. I didn't look away.

His agony was exquisite.

HELP ME! Addict mouthed. Then he stuck out his tongue and traced the letters against the canopy glass in reverse.

HELPME

Addict's ship was rejecting him. During acclimation, the drills had told us that was impossible. They said if you made it twenty-eight days inside your ship, she was yours forever.

They lied.

All I could do was shrug. What did Addict want me to do? Ram his ship with mine and kill us both? He was doomed, I was doomed. There was no escape.

During the mission briefing, Tsuros had warned the squadron not to attempt to fly out of the null-space bubble. He claimed that hitting the edge of the field was like flying into a black hole. A ship that hit the border would be ripped apart by the interaction between null-space and real space. Because we were inside an envelope of time compression, it would take a subjectively infinite amount of time for a ship that hit the border to disintegrate.

I can remember Tsuros' exact words:

"Sub-atomic pieces of you will be materializing along the flight path for billions of years. If you're lucky and go in headfirst, you might only be conscious for a hundred million years of it."

This might have been another lie, a fable to keep us from trying to escape. But I believed this one. There was a sacrosanct awe in the way Tsuros described the billion-year breakup. I think he recognized a suffering beyond anything he could personally inflict. He had to respect that. Addict painted more letters against his canopy with the point of his tongue.

HELP OR BOOM

I understood. Addict was threatening to deploy the bomb, here and now. I looked to the other pilots. Corrupt waved his hands, signing NO! Liar's jaw flapped uselessly. Murderess wasn't even watching. She stared emptily out her cockpit, a feverish cast to her skin. As usual, they were no help.

The green light in Addict's cockpit faded, the realignment window nearly closed. His face was piggish and insipid, with his nose smashed against the canopy. I stared into his eyes, desperate pools of dying light.

"DO IT," I signed back.

All was dark.

I had two hundred hours to wonder what it would be like to be blown up by a baryon bomb. Would I have time to see a flash of light? Would the bomb even generate light, or would they be anti-photons? I didn't know.

I kept turning to Addict's position, waiting for the doomsday flash. Tsuros hadn't briefed us on what would happen if one of us was crazy enough to pull the trigger halfway to the target.

It would kill us all, surely. But what next? Maybe the ripple would expand throughout null-space, killing every other ship in transit. Maybe it would blow a hole in the universe and flood ours with matter built on an entirely different set of physical laws. Perhaps the pillars of time themselves would collapse, trapping us all in an instant of antimatter annihilation for eternity.

It was useless to wonder, but I had nothing else to do. In the end, it didn't even matter. Whether through courage or cowardice, Addict never managed to detonate the bomb.

The eleventh alignment came at last, and Addict was dead. I stared at the distorted outline of his face, crushed against the canopy by his ship's heaving innards. A gory halo of dark, jammy clots floated around his head in the compression fluid. How he'd suffered!

As I gazed at his wretched face, I felt certain he must have tried to deploy the bomb. Was he too injured to perform the firing sequence? Maybe there was a timer to keep us from blowing ourselves up. Maybe he didn't even have a bomb. What if the Hezo only had enough material to make one? What if I was riding on top of it?

You're the only one who matters.

For the next five alignments, Addict's ship continued to bioluminesce as it drifted away from our formation. His light had taken on a sickly brown-yellow tone. On the sixth alignment, his ship failed to light. I couldn't see it out there in the dark, but it was too soon to have drifted out of the bubble. I think he killed his ship as he decomposed. Poison unto the end. So then, there were four.

But not for long. Murderess's condition continued to deteriorate. She had lost a great deal of weight, her face was skeletal. Her eyes were glazed over, and her skin was blotchy. She was dying.

Sometimes, she would be furious, beating against the canopy with her skinny fists. Sometimes, she would weep, covering her face with her hands to hide from us. Still, she managed to align her ship each time. No one wanted the billion-year death.

On the thirty-second alignment, Murderess didn't move. Her face was frozen in a rictus of suffering, and I suspected she was dead. On the thirty-third alignment, there was no doubt. For seven more alignments, I watched her rot, then her ship died, too. Then there were three of us, Liar, Corrupt, and I.

I confess, it took me much longer than it should have to realize what had probably killed Murderess. Thirty-three alignments at two hundred hours per. For several alignments afterward, I searched Corrupt's face, looking for some sign he knew. I saw only fear, he trembled all the time now. Like a rat.

Liar held better than Corrupt. During the alignments, he was alert and composed. Somehow, he'd managed to catch religion. Every alignment, he did a little ceremony where he held both palms together and nodded his head towards me. Then he would smile and draw a symbol on his canopy that had no meaning to me.

I felt uncomfortable when he did this. We were outside the bounds of the physical universe, yet I still couldn't escape the feeling there were *mijing* standing right behind us. In the old days, we would have both been executed for participating in religious delusions.

My own fears ebbed and flowed like the tide. Every time I thought I'd truly resigned myself to death, I would find a fresh layer of hope had sprouted beneath. I'd spend days stomping it out. Man is such a curious onion.

I had endless time for such idiot musings. I plumbed every crevice of my memory. I thought of Pirate and his sculptures. I thought of Tsuros and his crushing fingers. I remembered my capture on Keilu Five, the stunning feelings of loss and abandonment.

I dwelt on Murderess and her terrible fate. For several alignments after she died, I suffered intrusive thoughts. I had a sharp, insane desire to trigger the bomb and cleanse myself of what I'd seen. But they faded, like everything else.

The lights of the forty-fourth and final alignment dimmed. I drifted in the space womb, waiting to fly my impossible mission. Ready be reborn in fire, extinguished in an apocalyptic explosion.

I confess, I was eager.

摇落深知宋玉悲

风流儒雅亦吾师

怅望千秋一洒泪

萧条异代不同时

江山故宅空文藻

云雨荒台岂梦思

最是楚宫俱泯灭

舟人指点到今疑

20
THE WINGED MESSENGER

We were but a handful of black diamonds flung at the stars. Only three bombers emerged from null-space: Corrupt, Liar, and myself. Murderess and Addict had drifted into the fringe. Their remains would litter our path for an aeon. Our objective was ahead. At this distance, it was only a centimeter in diameter. Until this moment, I hadn't truly believed this could be our mission. It was too insane. Now, there was no denying it.

We were flying directly into a star.

Into a star!

Instinct compelled me to turn around, fire my reactor and retreat. To resist it, I peered ahead at the white dwarf and tried to identify our target. My canopy darkened as it lensed forward, protecting my eyes. Even at this great distance, the star could damage them. I was frail. I was insignificant. I was nothing. The star was enormous beyond comprehension. The only thing vaster was Tsuros' hubris for dreaming we could destroy it.

I couldn't yet see the Starmine. During approach, our orders were to fly quenched-and-clenched, with our reactors at nil output and no maneuvering. It was a tremendous effort of faith. Our path had been manually calculated by a Hezo navigator on the ringship. He had to hit a tiny mark on a rotating sphere more than a million kilometers in diameter from a distance of light years.

How many light years?

There was ample time to wonder. It would take many hours to reach the star. For a year in the dark, I had been trying to identify our target. Now that we had arrived at the system, there was more data I could use to try and solve the puzzle. I didn't know what multiple of C we'd accelerated to. If it was less than ten times the speed of light, I think the Hezo wouldn't have risked using the irreplaceable ringships. It would have been a carrier jump.

The squadron had performed forty-five alignments at two hundred hours per, so we'd been in flight for just over a year. Ten light years from our origin point, minimum. I started by considering the closest possible stars and figured up from there.

The drills never told us what system Ananke Station was hidden in, and I would have been executed for asking. I had to figure it out myself. During our training missions, I could sometimes make out stellar flares from a nearby star, a particularly cantankerous red dwarf. By itself, that hardly narrowed the possibilities. But during one training session, I saw two simultaneous flares. Our main star had a smaller, less luminous companion. That was the key to figuring it out.

My guess is those two red dwarfs were Andromedae GX and GQ. If I was right, it meant Ananke Station was in Groombridge 34. A system so remote and irrelevant the Hezo hadn't bothered to change its ancient vanity designation. It made perfect sense. Groombridge 34 was at the very limits of Hezo-controlled space, as far from the front as possible. Even in that utter backwater, they were still falling apart.

The power to change that was in my hands, the spur controls of my Yama 10 Bomber. I loosened my grip, careful not to activate the thrusters and give us away. My arms felt strong and awake. The anti-atrophy agents had done their work.

My legs weren't as solid. They were a cramping mess of pins and needles. As I stretched them out, my left big toe came in contact with something hard and unyielding amidst the ship-flesh. I ignored the sensation. I didn't trust myself to think about that yet.

I craned my head around the canopy, looking for more clues. If this was Rigel Kentarus, where were Toliman and Proxima Centauri? I felt a strange déjà vu. There was something oddly familiar about this system.

Then as I twisted my body to look behind us, I had my answer. A glittering silver disc, too bright to be a star. It was surrounded by the gossamer threads of an orbital lattice. Ship traffic made them appear to shimmer.

The Messenger!

The monster in my sights was Sol. Tsuros had sent us to destroy the sun.

For the long hours of approach, the revelation burned in my mind like stellar fusion. Mercury! Old Earth! Phobos! Europa, Cassini Station! The skeleton system, our depleted, forgotten homeland. A graveyard of barren rock, where every molecule of useful material had been stripped away and cast into the stars. With every bone picked, the Collaborators must have turned their gaze inward. They devoured Sol itself.

This Starmine was our target. The Collaborators had developed technology that allowed them to tunnel into stars so they could mine vast quantities of exotic materials at the moment of creation. During the briefing, we learned the Clabs had poured resources into this pilot Starmine for decades, stripping worlds and beggaring entire systems.

But the payoff!

Once the first Starmine was online, it would enable the construction of countless others. In a few short centuries, the Collaborators would be a Type II civilization. The Hezo Collective Prosperity Sphere would be as irrelevant to them as bacteria.

But the Collaborators had bet everything on this first Starmine. It seemed a safe bet. Who would dream the backward Hezo could invent a weapon capable of destroying a star? Tsuros told us if we could destroy the Starmine completely, the Collaborators would be ruined. In the chaos that followed, Hezo loyalists would rise from the ashes and overwhelm them.

One empire would fall, another would rise. I was riding on top of the bomb that could decide it all.

The power!

I felt it thrumming through my arms, resonating through my symbiotic husk of corybantic phase-diamond. The power to destroy a star if I could only make it to the target depth. It wasn't enough to simply fling bombs at the sun. We had to sneak inside the mine and detonate as deep as possible. If I wanted to bring the giant down, I needed to reach the tachocline.

Sol dominated my attention over the long approach, growing larger by the second. I became aware of a silvery thread running almost parallel to my flight path. At first, I thought perhaps it was a piece of debris from Addict or Murderess. As I squinted into the darkness, the canopy assisted my vision until I could resolve the links in the chain. They were individual ships.

The strand was a line made of thousands of freighters. Most were long, silvery cargo cylinders. There were also pill-shaped tankers, reefers bulging with cryo-machinery, and bony ore boats laden with unprocessed asteroids.

The freighters flew nose-to-tail in such perfect synchronization I thought they must be a star-train, with a linkage between each ship. But there was none, just a narrow gap between each vessel. I scanned along the line as it disappeared into the darkness. There was no beginning or end that I could see.

Holding my fist to the canopy as a reference, I guessed I was still more than ten million kilometers out from Sol. Surely, the line couldn't possibly stretch all the way to the Starmine, but I never saw a break in the chain.

As Sol swelled to occupy more and more of my canopy, I noticed more silver filaments. Each was another line of freighters. Soon, I could make out a great vortex of strands converging on the Starmine. I tried to calculate how many there were and how much cargo they might be carrying. The numbers were simply too big for me to hold in my head. I could only imagine hollowed-out moons and siphoned-up seas, a great dusty desert where the asteroid belt had once been.

As I gazed at this incredible display of organization, I was reminded of my time on Ananke Station. Tripping over tangled pneumatic lines and huddling with the others as we slowly froze to death in the dark. How did we ever dream we could fight this?

Ahead of me, the closest line of freighters had a subtle arc that crossed my path a hundred kilometers beneath me. I got a feel for the incredible speed of insertion as I passed seven or eight ships each second. We were coming in so hot! A shudder of excitement ran through my shoulders. I would suffer tremendously during deceleration.

Ahead, a dark shape eclipsed the sun. My breath caught as I recognized it from our silhouette training. A Collaborator Kulan B-type destroyer, moving into an intercept course.

I tightened my grip on the spurs. The reactor blazed, and my Yama pulsed to life around me.

Time to die.

生涯岂料承优诏，世事空知学醉歌。
江上月明胡雁过，淮南木落楚山多。
寄身且喜沧洲近，顾影无如白发何。
今日龙钟人共老，媿君犹遣慎风波。

21
狗屎

During the briefing, Tsuros was adamant: we were not to fire our reactors until we reached the corona. We were to trust in our field generators, which would render us virtually invisible. Quenched and clenched, those were our orders.

Goshi. I doubted we were anything near invisible. I broke my orders and fired my reactor. Out of the corner of my eye, I saw a black whorl gliding by, the faintest stress on the fabric of nothing. Corrupt had abandoned the order even faster than I had. I diverted hard and followed him. Compression fluid hardened around me like cement.

I glanced back, expecting to see Liar following us. There was no sign of him. I wondered if, perhaps, he really was invisible. But then, I saw the faint smear of his Yama streaking across space. Liar never fired his reactor. He followed his orders, right into the side of the destroyer. His Yama vanished in a silent flare, and I clenched my jaw, awaiting annihilation.

There was no all-consuming conflagration. The baryon bomb had not deployed. Had Liar died in null-space or simply given up? I had no time to wonder. Our presence was no longer a secret.

I gripped the spurs and throttled up. For a year, I had touched these controls only once every two hundred hours for alignment. Now, I could cry havoc and let slip the throttle of my bomber.

I was free! I could fly!

I had drilled so long for this moment. My veins sang with euphoria as the reactor burned brighter, infusing my ship with power. The compression fluid thrummed against my eardrums in time with my pulse.

I was immune to most of the first-battle pitfalls. My mouth couldn't go dry, it was flooded with compression fluid. If I soiled myself, it didn't matter, I was cathed and tubed up. The ship had been a part of me for a year, and I knew every gurgle and throb as intimately as the beating of my own heart. I was ready. I rocketed forward, bound for the sun.

Corrupt raced ahead of me. Even though I knew he was there, I could barely keep eyes on him. When I tried to focus on his ship, his outline rolled out of my vision like a floater.

"Lose sight, lose fight!"

I must have heard Tsuros say that a hundred times. I killed thrust and sent my bomber in a transverse-longitudinal roll, doing a quick sweep for potential threats.

Behind us, the Collaborator destroyer turned ponderously, like a drunk wheeling about to see who'd thrown something. Liar's suicide was just a pinprick in the side of the behemoth. The Kulan class was obsolete by several generations. They were tiny compared to Hezo destroyers. But this Crossfire was still a hundred times larger than our bombers, heavily armored, and bristling with guns.

Streams of glittering tinsel issued from the turrets, turning golden in the sunlight. I was stupidly captivated. The barrage was almost too pretty for me to recognize it as a threat.

FLAK!

Each filament of light was a streaking cluster bomb. The destroyer couldn't draw a bead on our stealthed bombers, so it was blanketing space with its anti-missile defenses. I whipped my ship back towards the sun so fast I nearly knocked myself out.

When my head cleared, I saw I'd overcorrected. It was too late to change course. I could only hammer the throttle forward, riding it until my vision grayed out. I was determined I would either outrun the flak or be unconscious when it killed me.

Ahead of me, Corrupt had the same idea. He burned so hard I could see the orange-red rings of his thrusters, glaring through the field effect like a pair of angry eyes. As I diverted, I passed through his vapor trail, and my ship flinched at the momentary touch of superheated gas. My Yama was in for a rude awakening if we survived to reach the corona.

A thousand golden motes exploded, flooding space with a static storm of shrapnel. Flying directly away from the destroyer, Corrupt was safe. Golden sparks raced ahead of my ship, the shell's most energetic outliers. I was in range! A single touch was death. I rammed the throttle forward to the limit.

It felt like my body was being crushed in a giant's fist. The diaphragm-assist kept pumping, but I couldn't breathe. I told myself to hold thrust for a ten-count, but I couldn't remember what came after seven. Everything became confused.

I'm not sure if I managed to throttle down or if the Yama simply couldn't continue. I floated on the edge of unconsciousness, my head a balloon, inflating and deflating with each pulse. I strained my ears for the telltale hiss of fluid escaping through a punctured carapace. I only heard my reactor, pinging with thermal stress.

I was alive!

I had a few moments to buzz with adulation as my heart fought to get blood back into my brain. I'd outrun the flak! But the gauntlet had only begun. I was soaring along the endless lines of freighters, bound for the Starmine.

Corrupt had flown so far ahead of me, his thrusters were only pinpricks. If I wanted to catch up, I would have to go full burn.

Let them take the hits. Tsuros' voice rang in my ears.

I had intended all along to defy him and race ahead on my own. But it hadn't worked out that way. The others were all gone, and now, Corrupt had panicked. He plummeted ahead with his jets wide open, showing his ass to the destroyer. I knew he was a dead man.

The fool would draw Diyu down on both of us. I needed to get out of the line of fire. With my nose pointed at Sol, I accelerated until I heard the rumble of my own jets kicking in. I burned for a few seconds, giving the destroyer's gunners time to plot my trajectory.

I cut throttle, and let the field generator kick in. Then I engaged vertical thrust and leaned towards a silver line of freighters. My plan was to hide behind the endless train of ships so the destroyer couldn't track my silhouette against the sun.

But I'd made an error. I'd gauged the distance to the freighters, expecting them to be the same size as Hezo supply ships. These solar freighters were far larger than even the UNESECA freighters. They must have been thirty kilometers long! I was only halfway to the line when the destroyer launched the next salvo.

The first shell exploded, perhaps a hundred clicks ahead of my ship. Watching the flak pattern, I realized the gunners on the destroyer were supercharging their mass drivers. The flak guns were meant to destroy missiles coming in, not bombers flying out. The golden motes were hurled with so much force they exploded in cones, glittering gouts of dragon's breath. The next shell burst even closer than the last. My ruse hadn't worked! Somehow, they had a bead on me.

Speed was more important than stealth now. I gave the thrusters more power, veering into a series of gut-twisting turns. The temperature inside my cockpit fluctuated from freezing to searing. My exchangers struggled to cope with the rapid shifts in output. My Yama ripped through space, executing a twisting series of arcs that were less maneuvers and more sheer panic.

I couldn't shake them. My eyes locked on a golden streak flying towards me. I felt a strange calm, certain it was the last thing I'd ever see. But the shell flew past me, less than five hundred meters from my Yama's nose. My body went rigid, as if that would help.

If the shell popped, I was a dead man, but it sailed on, bound for the sun. The canopy lens telescoped as I tracked the fleeting bomb, and then I could see a rippling shadow, twin rings of burning jets.

I wasn't the target. The cluster bomb scored a direct hit, dragon's fire scouring Corrupt's ship. At the very limits of canopy magnification, the black diamond of his bomber disintegrated into shards of corybantic-phase confetti. Then everything went black.

I thought the baryon bomb had killed me, but the familiar sounds of my ship said otherwise. Corrupt's reactor had exploded. My canopy had gone opaque to keep it from blinding me.

"Thank you!" I *blubbed* into the compression fluid. The ship couldn't understand, but it needed to be said.

My canopy cleared, and I shot towards the freighters, eyes alert for the sparkle of shrapnel. My mind burned as hot as my jets. No bomb! Corrupt's ship had been sliced to ribbons. The antimatter containment field would have surely been breached.

Liar's crash should have annihilated the destroyer and everything else for a thousand kilometers. Back in the bubble, Addict had been on the edge of madness when he threatened to deploy. He hadn't been too afraid to trigger. He was sitting on a dud.

Did the Hezo only have enough antimatter for one bomb? Was I the only one? Was this whole thing just Tsuros' sick idea of a joke?

I didn't have long to think about it. I sped towards the silver line as shells exploded all around me. Suddenly, my canopy was full of golden sparks. I braced for the killing crack of shrapnel, but my luck held. My reactor roared, my thrusters howled, and I shot behind the freighters and decelerated.

It was agony, like my body was being crushed in a hydraulic press. The blurred line of freighters resolved into individual ships as I braked. I'd hoped the Clabs wouldn't risk firing on their own men, but the bombardment continued.

I realized why. The freighters were unmanned! They had no cockpits, only the thin stalks of sensor-arrays. Of course, they were automated. It should have been obvious, but I'd spent so long under the Hezo boot I'd forgotten such things were possible.

The destroyer blasted indiscriminately, peppering the line of freighters with a steady hail of flak. I fought to keep the twisting silver line between me and the destroyer, terrified something would make it through the narrow gap between each freighter. *How in Diyu were they still on top of me?* I was field-stealthed, zero-sum, full-organic. Somehow, the gunners on the Crossfire had a constant lock on my position.

I stubbed my toe on the answer. My secret weapon! I had given us away and gotten Corrupt and Liar both killed. My turn was next. I'd outrun the flak, but the destroyer had more cards to play. The artillerymen on the Crossfire switched guns and raked the line with their quad-linked chain driver.

Several ships ahead of me was a skeleton barge, a spindly ribcage hauling captured asteroids. A spray of white-hot iridium rails lanced through the chunks of nickel-iron like a fork through blueberry gelatin. At first, I was relieved they were off target, but then I realized they weren't aiming at me. They'd turned the space in front of me into a minefield of debris!

I wrenched the Yama into a desperate spiral, pushing my ship harder than I'd ever dared before. The bomber's innards pulsed around me with the same urgency, mirroring my adrenaline shakes. The Yama weren't sentient, the drills told us they were no smarter than a mantis or a beetle. Still, my ship was a living thing. It could feel my terror and it didn't want to die.

On this, we were in full agreement. I piloted my bomber in a crazy corkscrew, dodging the railgun rain. The sun loomed larger, and the shots flew wider. I was outrunning the barrage!

My canopy grew darker, the sun swallowed the other stars.

Thou shalt have no other gods before me.

The real terror began.

剑外忽传收蓟北
初闻涕泪满衣裳
却看妻子愁何在
漫卷诗书喜欲狂
白日放歌须纵酒
青春作伴好还乡
即从巴峡穿巫峡
便下襄阳向洛阳

22
BRINGER OF JOLLITY

No words can capture the utter insignificance I felt. The sun bloomed to cover half of my canopy. I was a flea, a speck, a subatomic nothing. The entire output of my life wasn't even a spark against the omniflame.

Sol.

The primordial titan. My ancestors were forged from Sol's body and incubated by Sol's radiance. No matter how far we scattered across the stars, our birthstar's substance would remain within us, atoms that would endure until the end of the universe.

I accelerated, trying to get as much distance as possible from the destroyer. Hurtling along the silver line of freighters, I saw the pockmark on the face of God. The Starmine. There were nine brilliant points of light arranged in a ring, flickering artificial stars that sometimes outshone the sun. It was an affront, a monstrous arrogance. But I had come for a far greater hubris.

Invisible to the naked eye, the corona appeared through my canopy filters as a seething red-violet storm. The lashing prominences were dark garnet, the hot spots ranging from madder to vermillion. Those swells might be three million degrees, a flare could be twenty million.

This section of the Starmine was a series of ring-shaped megastructures that generated a magnetic funnel. The first ring was at the outermost fringe of the corona, a five-hundred-kilometer-wide band of gleaming silver. I'd been briefed that the ring diameters would contract as I approached the sun.

At the chromosphere, the Starmine was only a hundred kilometers wide. There was no data on what would happen when I was inside the star. My orders were to wing it. Judging with my fist against the canopy, I was approximately ninety minutes away from the first ring.

The temperature rose in my cockpit. I could hear my exchangers singing with effort, creating a *basso profundo* duet that rang in my bones. I pushed the throttle forward, and the Yama shuddered with relief. A moment later, I was crushed by an unexpected burst of acceleration. If I weren't in an effective vacuum, I might have thought I'd broken through the sound barrier.

The sudden shift veered me off course. I tried to pitch down and nearly murdered myself. What was meant to be a minor correction wrenched me straight into a collision course with the freighters below.

I barely managed to choke up in time. The violent motion gave me a micro-blackout. I had to tense my legs and abdomen to stay conscious, gulping compression fluid in a hick maneuver. When the danger passed, I had the terrible feeling my eyeballs were about to burst. I hesitated to touch the controls, afraid the next motion might knock me unconscious. I'd forgotten this was supposed to happen. The Yama soaked up more energy than it could eliminate with its exchangers. It had switched from thrusters to RAMP.

"It'll be an adjustment, but there's no way to simulate it without flying into a star. Adapt," Tsuros had warned us.

The adjustment was like flying an entirely new ship. The spurs had become hypersensitive to my slightest motion. All my instincts were now wrong by an order of magnitude.

The Yama 10 Bomber was a strange design for a stranger purpose. Ordinarily, it wouldn't make sense to fit a one-man bomber with radiative maneuvering planes. They were energy-hungry, far too powerful for such a tiny mass. RAMP was meant for capital ships, like the destroyer on my tail.

But there was nothing ordinary about flying into a star. The idea was to use RAMP as a set of super-exchangers, converting vast quantities of surplus heat into thrust. For the entire year-long jaunt through null-space, my Yama had been an energy miser, loath to waste a single erg. Inside the corona, I was so flush with power it would literally burn a hole in my pocket if I didn't spend it.

I needed to get distance from the freighters, some space around me so I could get my bearings. I tried to lift up gently, but even my most delicate motion was too hasty. The bomber sprang like a cricket, spinning wildly. Another near-blackout, more hick-gulping.

When I came around, my neck felt like a can crushed beneath a boot. The canopy strobed between sun and space. I was in a death-spin that would have incapacitated any human with an ordinary vestibular system. Thanks to my surgery, I could bear it, but it was still disorienting.

I couldn't feel my extremities. For a few terrifying seconds, I was afraid I'd severed my spine. Paresthesia came first, then pain. I began to feel my hands again, and I wriggled my toes. Again, my left foot struck the foreign body. My big gamble. My last resort was still lodged in the fold by my left foot. *Not yet.*

Delicate as a surgeon, I eased my ship out of the spin. I positioned my tail to the sun and my nose to the black as if I could hide what I was doing from Sol. Control sensitivity had become more reasonable, the Yama recalibrating on the fly. Facing out at the emptiness of space, I could admit it to myself. I was terrified of Sol. I was afraid to fly into the Starmine.

I didn't have to. I could detonate right here. The explosion would wreck a hundred thousand freighters and wipe out the destroyer that had killed Liar and Corrupt. But the Sun would endure, and the collaborators would rebuild. History would remember me as the greatest premature ejaculator of all time.

No. I wouldn't go out like that. I wanted to find a way out of this without killing anyone else. I realized the Yama was uniquely positioned to pull off an Oberth maneuver. The hotter I got, the more thrust I could generate. I could slingshot around the sun, attain an incredible velocity, and fire myself into deep space.

Perhaps I could even catch a glimpse of Old Earth or the Jupiter Pentakis on my way into interstellar space. I was captivated by the idea, but it was a fantasy. An Oberth maneuver required exact calculations I couldn't possibly perform. I would just burn up.

If I was going to go out that way, I wanted to go bigger: fire all my guns at once and explode into space. I could push RAMP as hard as it could go and suicide from acceleration alone. My funeral pyre would be a vast antimatter wound on the surface of Sol. If I was going to go that far, why not go all the way?

I know what you are. I know you won't fail me.

My eyes narrowed. Sergeant Tsuros was light years away, and I still couldn't escape him. Because he was right. I couldn't resist the challenge, the risk, the *glory*. I could run the gauntlet. I could be the one.

I could destroy the sun.

I turned the Yama's nose back towards the task. As Sol's golden face loomed large in my canopy, I saw a glimmer of light at the corner of my vision. At first, I thought it was only wayward flak, but then six more flashes followed. They fired in sequence.

My canopy lensed forward to assist, telescoping until I could make out the spherical profile of a Collaborator capital ship. The Yama's innards shuddered against me, reacting to my mounting dread.

Hexagons ringing pentagons. It was a Glömer class carrier. Those seven flashes were interceptors!

I pressed my thumb against the canopy and calculated, gauging the relative distance of the carrier as I'd been trained.

I was struck by the insanity of my position. Facing against a squadron of Collaborator interceptors, my only hope to gauge their vector was a guesstimate with my thumb. They were headed for the first ring of the Starmine, and it looked like they might beat me there. That was trouble.

The Collaborators would have the sun at their backs, and they could set up a defensive formation and pick me off as I tried to fly through. I was unarmed except for a weapon that would kill us all. My only hope was to outrun them.

Could I do that? The fighters would have an initial burst from their launch catapults, but I doubted the Collaborators would do anything as harebrained as fitting RAMP on a one-man ship. I pushed the Yama as hard as I dared. Then I pushed it a little further.

I was getting a better sense of the newfound power at my disposal. The exchangers roared, and the ship's innards rumbled with strain. I soared towards the sun, running a race for my life.

Gray crept in at the edges of my vision. My circulatory system couldn't keep up with the acceleration. I backed off the throttle slightly, and the taste of copper flooded my mouth. I wondered if my heart had given out.

Instead, there was a pleasant tingle running up my left arm. It reached my chest and exploded outward, sparkling in my fingertips. The Yama had sensed my low blood-oxygen level and was administering Djamori.

The drug took hold. My vision sharpened, outlines leaping out at me as if they'd been honed. Objects moved with a new fluidity, and I could react faster. The polling rate had increased for all of my nerves. Strength flooded into my arms and legs, an explosive potential that begged to be tested.

I could understand why Addict had ruined himself for this. If I wasn't careful, it would ruin me, too. I was hyper-fixating on the feeling of the spurs in my hands, the contented purr of the exchangers, and the *stringendo* drumroll of my heart.

The first ring of the Starmine was approximately fifteen minutes ahead. At full telescope of my canopy, I could see the details clearly. The ring was a torus wreathed with tetrahedral spines radiating from the outer edge at forty-degree intervals. It looked like a spiked collar.

Suspended above each of the nine spires was a pure black orb, what I'd thought were artificial stars. Occasionally, they flared to life, so bright my whole canopy would wince into near-opacity. The spheres were only tiny dots at this distance, they were no more than a hundred meters in diameter. As I drew closer, I could see their effect on the corona was incredible.

Each orb was the origin of a vast, teardrop-shaped magnetic tempest: a million-degree hurricane that stretched out for hundreds of kilometers. I looked upon the ninefold storm and comprehended a pattern.

Farther into the corona, each storm was replicated, doubling in size. This continued, again and again until the pattern was too faint to see. In the eddies between each storm, there were echoes of the whole in microcosm, endlessly repeating self-similarity. The sun-stabilizing spheres had created a fractal the size of Jupiter.

An unfamiliar sound rose in my ship, I thought some system must have failed. I was that system. I was screaming, and I couldn't stop. It was a low, drowned keening, pitched down by the compression fluid in my voice box.

I was gripped by a powerful urge to take the spurs and fly right into one of the freighters. Anything to get this awful realization out of my head. This was more than monstrous, it was blasphemous. Tai Di had grown powerful beyond anything I'd dared dream.

As my mind plunged into mortal terror, my body took the chance to rebel. My hand pulled the throttle without conscious decision, preparing to divert and flee. Deceleration throbbed in my teeth.

As I slowed, the streaking silver rails resolved into individual ships again. The lines of freighters converged at the ring, a hundred trains zippering together from every direction. It was like a wire stranding machine, twisting together a cable of ships out of thousands of freighters at incredible speed. Trillions upon trillions of kilotons of cargo flowed all around me, bound for the Starmine. I gulped at my doom like a witless goldfish.

It's the drug!

The insistent significance of every detail was overloading my brain and compromising my decision-making. I couldn't possibly run. There was a destroyer on my tail, and I was flying too fast to divert before I hit the corona. If I had any wits, I would have tried to surrender. But I was hyperventilating and probably in tachycardia.

I let go of the spurs, squeezed my hands into tight fists, and closed my eyes. I forced myself to breathe slowly. The respiration-assist thumped my chest off-kilter, like a dance partner who'd missed a step.

I was able to regain control of myself, but my moment of cowardice cost me dearly. Now, the attack wing was going to beat me to the ring. Cockpit temperature was rising, my exchangers groaning with complaint. I had to fly faster. I throttled up, hastening to my doom.

Ahead, I caught a glimpse of a banking interceptor. The ship was delta-shaped. Its nose came to a needle point, and its tail was a shark's-tooth curve of thruster banks. The titanium-white hull caught the sunlight with a fierce glow. The ship's canopy was ruby red, the muzzles of its four cannons were crimson. Two blue cheek blazes just under the canopy were the last piece of the puzzle. It was an AGA\LAG 81. I could almost hear Tsuros bark, "*Affirmative!*" at me.

Paranoia set in. Why were there only seven of them? Why had there only been a single destroyer guarding the approach? It was almost insulting. Did the Collaborators really think so little of us?

Why shouldn't they? They'd already killed Corrupt and Liar. If I couldn't out-fly seven interceptors, I was next.

来顾鸟树巅惧指恶冥慕

上敢翠珠木丸人神冥所

海不双三珍金患逼遊何

鸿潢见在矫无服明我者

孤池侧巢矫得美高今弋

23
THE SWAN

Seven to one, sixty seconds to the ring. The djamori in my veins whispered that the AGA\LAG 81 interceptors were nothing and that I was invincible! But the rest of my body was not in accord. My scrotum retracted, my chute tightened around the output pipe. My hands were poised to wrench at the controls and fly back the way I'd come. My cowardice was opposed by Tsuros' ghost, screaming in my ear:

"Dicta Six! *If you get caught, fly at the danger!*"

How fast could the Yama really go? How much acceleration could my body withstand? There was only one way to find out. I took a deep breath, filling my lungs with compression fluid. Then I hammered down. *Full throttle.*

I was crushed into the flesh of the Yama, and my weight doubled, then quadrupled. My body was a lump of pure suffering, amplified by djamori hyperawareness.

I was flying directly into the sun. My canopy had grown as dark as welding glass. Ten seconds from the ring, I could only see outlines. Pinpricks of light flickered from the waiting interceptors.

They fired at me!

The AGA/LAG 81s had been designed to protect their carrier by shooting down incoming missiles. I was no missile! With leaden hands, I twisted the spurs, heedless of the pain. I darted behind a line of freighters like a squirrel hiding on the far side of a tree. The shots flew wide. They hadn't expected me to be so nimble. I wanted to smile, but my grimace was too heavy.

Dicta three: *Fire only at close range, and only when your opponent is properly in your sights.*

My Yama flew faster than anything they'd ever seen. They still fired, but I was already upon them. Our paths crossed for a microsecond that felt like forever. I strained my ears against the screaming reactor, listening for the crack of doom against my diamond hull.

They missed!

But then, a flash of titanium white at three-o-clock caught my eye. The seventh interceptor! He'd waited in reserve, holding his fire until I was in killing range. The djamori screamed in my veins, time dripped by in heartbeats. My canopy lensed towards the ruby gleam of his cockpit, a viper's eye. I clenched the spurs for my final gamble, remembering the moment when RAMP first kicked in. I had to wait until the instant before he fired.

Twin cannons flashed. I was a heartbeat faster, ramming my spurs into a spine-crushing vertical juke. My Yama sprang like a flea, bounding above the spray of tungsten slugs. My battered brain was crushed against the roof of my skull once more, and my vision flared white-orange.

It hurt so bad, I wished I'd just let him shoot me. The interceptor pilot fired his jets and gave chase. He had me in his sights, but I was flying faster than his bullets.

Celeritas sum!

I laughed into the fluid, half-crazed with djamori and adrenaline. I'd outrun them all! Then the space around my ship erupted with energy, coruscating rays of dazzling violet-green light. Polyphasic beams! A purple nova burst against my canopy, and everything went black.

I clenched my jaw, preparing to disintegrate. Instead, I felt pressure at the back of my head. More acceleration. I hurtled even faster.

It was just dumb luck. At this range, the polyphasic beam couldn't penetrate my phase-diamond skin. Praise the inverse square law! My exchangers drank up the beam's energy gladly, converting it into thrust.

I was flying blind. My canopy was still blacked out, and I was afraid it had been damaged. Eventually, the Yama let light in, facing the sun with a drunkard's reluctance. We screamed into the Starmine, surrounded by silver rails that vanished into infinity.

My chest hurt, and I was acutely aware I was underwater. Even in the throes of a djamori high, I was drowning in G-force. Satisfied I'd found the absolute limit, I eased off the throttle. Color crept back into my vision, and terrible cramps racked my body. Everything hurt, but I was alive. I could feel myself becoming more lucid with each heartbeat.

I had to work up the courage to check my six. Yawing backward, I could see the seven tiny candles of their jets in hopeless pursuit. Without RAMP, they could never catch me. Without compression fluid, they would be torn apart in the attempt. I was free! It was an insane way for a man strapped to a bomb to feel, but I felt it anyway.

Sol grew ever-larger as I sailed across five million kilometers of corona. The rings whipped by, and I had time to ponder the filament cavity they maintained. The interval between rings shrank as I flew deeper, and the pitch of my exchangers climbed. As the corona became more energetic, more rings were needed to keep its fury at bay.

A million kilometers out, Sol filled my canopy completely. This was my cue to begin deceleration. I had reached the limit of our intel. The Hezo didn't know what was inside the Starmine, or if the Yama 10s could survive entry. My orders were to do whatever I could to try and reach the tachocline. If my ship failed, I was to deploy the baryon bomb.

It would be a delicate balance. If I was too slow, I would

overwhelm my exchangers and burn up. If I flew too fast, Icarus.

During the long deceleration, I wondered if anyone else had gotten this far. I realized I might be closer to the sun than any human being had ever been. Through my canopy, I watched world-swallowing gouts of plasma arc into the corona as dark rivers of relative-cool wove through burning oceans of swaying spicules.

What incomprehensible power! How vast, how eternal! Yet, somewhere beneath my awe, a voice whispered I was the one who could end it all. I'd outlived the others, outflown the destroyer, outrun the interceptors.

What would my last words be?

Semper Solus? Let there be night? Will the last surviving prisoner please turn off the sun?

I blinked at the insipid tenor of my own thoughts. The vertical jukes must have given me brain damage. My head was full of nervous babbling. I was afraid, stung by the scope of the sun. I was flying into the mouth of a monster. This ifrit was large enough to swallow every human being who'd ever lived, everything we'd ever built, and every planet we'd ever set foot on.

I was drugged to the gills, scourged with deceleration agony, and quivering with terror. I loved every moment of it. I had arrived.

仙台初见五城楼
风物凄凄宿雨收
山色遥连秦树晚
砧声近报汉宫秋
疏松影落空坛静
细草香闲小洞幽
何用别寻方外去
人间亦自有丹丘

24
The Works of the Lord are great, sought out of all them that have pleasure therein

I have seen what no one else has seen. I alone dared to enter the sun and gaze within. My bomber shot through the transition region in an ultraviolet blink.

The chromosphere bathed me in darkroom washes of crimson and rose-colored light. The photosphere was a butterfly, tickling my nose with fluttering rainbows and scintillating wisps. Prominences swelled and spicules danced. I peered out through the canopy in silent awe. I wanted to remember this for the rest of my life. There wouldn't be much more of it.

I soared into the convection zone. The Starmine's rings were spaced roughly two seconds apart, holding back a dense ocean of boiling plasma. There were so many rings! The great freighter fleet must have chewed the inner planets into husks. Perhaps even Jupiter's core had been tapped, bent into the silver ribs of the *dag gadol*.

Beyond the magna-walls, the substance of the sun boiled towards the photosphere. I was in the Rayleigh realm of the convection zone where Bénard cells billowed into thousand-kilometer steeples. My mind kept latching onto forms, trying to insist there must be some meaning, some function to the infinite instability.

I was captivated by the dancing plasma and didn't notice I was in danger until I almost collided with a freighter. The giant ship was just meters beneath my Yama's belly. I thought I must have drifted down into the line of freighters, but I was flying level. The freighter had broken away from the others. It climbed on a course that would crush me against the magnetic wall.

It was a ludicrous matchup. The freighter was almost three kilometers wide. It was an ocean of gleaming metal, rising to swallow my ship. In a fit of claustrophobic panic, I changed course abruptly and rammed the throttle.

The Yama shuddered in complaint, but I was too keyed-up to feel pain.

I was such a fool! How could I have let something so massive sneak up on me? I didn't let off the throttle. I had an illogical fear I would look back and find the freighter right on top of me.

Why had it flown off course? Did it malfunction?

I could visualize the wayward freighter crashing into a ring, collapsing the tunnel, drowning me in a wave of plasma. I found the courage to look back.

It was following me! The freighter's nose was pointed directly at my ship, and it wasn't alone. The once-rigid lines of freighters wavered. Dozens of ships diverged from their orderly ranks and closed in on me.

The master of this place had decided I'd gone far enough. Freighters flew into my path and converged all around me. A single brush with one of those hulks was instant death. I had a vision of my bomber crushed between two freighters, the phase-diamond hull popping like a glass ornament.

I had to escape! I accelerated, dipping between two ships trying to bar my way. Beyond them, there was a shrinking triangle between three intersecting giants. I shot through, bracing for the peal of shattering diamond. I made it unscathed, but a tangle of ships waited on the other side.

The Starmine had become a train-wrecked pandemonium of freighters. Yet, the chaos was coordinated and purposeful. The enormous freighters passed within meters of each other, but they never made contact. It was getting harder to find a way through.

There was a dark blot ahead where freighters arranged themselves into an impassible wall. I understood now. This obstacle course was meant to slow me down and force me to stop.

How many rings had I passed?

I was nowhere near the tachocline. If I deployed, the mission would fail. The wall of ships was coming up fast. I needed to decelerate.

I didn't.

I maintained speed, hurtling towards the wall. At the point of no return, I angled my nose at the narrow junction between two freighters. They were barely a meter apart. Though the Yama couldn't possibly fit, I rolled sideways to try and slip through. If I was wrong, it would be a quick death.

I wasn't wrong. At the last possible second, the two freighters lurched apart, permitting me to pass. I flew through the wall, giddy with fright. I knew it! The automatic freighters could neither kill me, nor could they allow me to kill myself. I exploded with short-sighted joy.

At once, the freighters seemed to realize they'd been found out, and they abandoned the tactic. The jumbled ships resumed their orderly lines. I had been flying along these ships for hours, but the way they moved in perfect unison still unnerved me. Soon, they were all back in place as if nothing had happened. I knew they couldn't harm me, but I still felt uneasy. They were just too damn big.

☼

I continued to descend. Deeper inside the Starmine, the tunnel flared into a spherical chamber. I slowed so I would have more time to react.

The chamber was a thousand kilometers wide, with tunnels branching off in every direction. At the center was a featureless black orb, one of the sun-stabilizing spheres. The orb was a nexus of activity. Lines of freighters flew close, and then whipped into a new direction, rocketing into one of the tunnels that branched off from the chamber. The streams of ships interlocked. Freighters fired away as fast and precise as bullets shooting between propeller blades. If only old Oswald Boelcke could see this!

I gave the sphere the widest possible berth, flying along the outer wall of the junction. Anything that could fling the freighters around like toys would surely destroy me. It was a wise choice. Even at the outermost edge of the chamber, the gravitational pull from the dark sphere was immense. I had to push the throttle until my exchangers wailed to make it through the junction.

What the hell was that sphere? Some sort of hyperon-vortex? A micro-singularity? Whatever it was, I hoped I wouldn't encounter others.

As I flew deeper into the convection zone, I saw immense forms beyond the magna-wall. These were megastructures, obscured by currents of rising plasma. My eyes were drawn by a massive black spire, which rose from a ring to thrust into a supercell. The spire was an axle.

Along its length, spokes twisted in the current. Each terminated in a plume of whip-like antennae. The strands danced and writhed in the roiling plasma with such intensity I wondered if they were alive. Were they sensors? Was it some kind of plasmic dynamo? I could only guess. I continued to fly alongside the mute freighters in a state of continual awe.

There was no sun-stabilizing sphere at the next junction. Leading up to it was a group of three rings. They were joined by the roots of three colossal silver structures that looked like cubist interpretations of trees.

I slowed for a closer look, paying a terrible price for opposing the pull of the core. My weight doubled, then tripled. It was a terrible reminder this was a one-way ride. My body could not possibly bear the strain it would take to escape.

The upper branches of Triggdrasil extended deep into the rivers of plasma. High in the branches, there were crystalline spheres swaying in the current. Through patches of less-dense plasma, I sometimes saw swirls of multicolored motes glittering inside. I had a childish moment of delight, imagining they were fruit from the galaxy tree. I wanted to linger, but gravity was ever-insistent.

As I delved deeper, I remained wary of trickery from the freighters. When the lines slowed abruptly, my hands were already poised on the spurs, ready to evade. The freighters braked hard. Shock ripples raced through their hulls. Ahead of us, other ships accelerated. A large gap formed.

It had to be a trap. I gunned it and continued into the empty section. Then an unusual movement outside the mine caught my eye.

A dark line formed in the convection cell beyond the wall. The filament cavity whirled out of control and became a cyclone. Burning wind hammered the magna-walls, which shuddered under the onslaught. I hit the throttle, but it was too late.

Like a cracking whip, Leviathan's tail lashed against the Starmine. Bolts of brilliant lighting arced in all directions. I winced, and the canopy phased opaque momentarily.

The magna-wall breached, and a torrent of plasma jetted into the Starmine. If I had been in its direct path, I would have been vaporized. Instead, my ship was struck by overspray and thrown into a terrible spin. I fought with the spurs, but they would not respond. The Yama shuddered in pain as we were blasted towards the opposite wall. I kept fighting the controls, expecting to crash at any moment.

Then the ship stopped spasming, and I regained control. I was able to pull out of the spin and re-orient. After I pulled up, my eyes shot to the breach, wondering what had saved me.

An enormous shadow deflected the plasma stream. One of the freighters had flown into the breach! The enormous ship melted like wax, burning in a flare of brilliant blue light.

The freighter sacrificed itself to save me! I'd ignored the warning when they all slowed. I felt a pang of guilt, though I knew they were just autonomous machines. Hordes of spidery robots issued from the nearest ring, linking together in chains and swarming around the dying freighter. I wanted to watch them repair the magna-wall, but I was flying away too fast.

My Yama was hurt. Its insides pulsed and shook, kneading me like dough. All I could do was try to go limp. Too well, I remembered the ballooning agony on Addict's face and the remains of Toucher gurgling out of the hatch. I took a beating, but the tremors subsided. I felt a twinge of senseless pride. I had always thought my Yama was a little tougher than the others.

I continued to descend. Now that I knew breaches could happen, I couldn't stop peering through the walls, flinching at the slightest flicker. The Starmine had seemed so monumental. I'd never dreamed it could fail, and now, it felt as if the whole thing might collapse at any time.

I realized I was being drawn in. The Starmine could have ended me at any time. The sun-stabilizing sphere could have ripped me to shreds. The freighters pulled their punches and let me slip past. Instead of crushing me, they had warned me. One even sacrificed itself to save me. What was this place? Why was it luring me in?

I had a long way down to think about it.

凤凰台上凤凰游
凤去台空江自流
吴宫花草埋幽径
晋代衣冠成古邱
三台半落青山外
二水中分白鹭洲
总为浮云能蔽日
长安不见使人愁

25

... − − − ...

The green alignment light came on.

I was surprised and touched when my cockpit bioluminesced. It felt like an unexpected visit from an old friend. The glow meant I had arrived at the tachocline. My long journey was over at last.

I began my final deceleration, wanting to savor my last moments inside of a star. Theoretically, I could equalize thrust with the pull of the core and linger forever. But in practice, I would weigh something like fifteen hundred kilograms. My organs would fail within minutes. I subjected my body to as much gravity as I could bear and watched the freighters gliding by.

I was still falling, past the endless shimmering jets that fueled the convection zone. I gazed at the long fingers of flame, adorned with shock-diamonds that pulsed in time with the magnetic heartbeat of the core. I was in the cathedral now, beneath the intertidal vault, where the rolling boil of the convection zone split from the radiative zone's serene sea.

Dividing the tachocline was a mega-ring, many times larger and thicker than the others. The outward facing edge was studded with thousands of pyramids. Atop each pyramid was a sun-stabilizing sphere. Nine enormous silver spires rose from the mega-ring and extended deep into the burning haze. They stretched into endless white-hot lines.

Were those physical cables? Beams of coherent light? Perhaps I was looking at the foundation of the entire Starmine: a toroidal anchor borne on Ferraro isorotation. I was only making uneducated guesses. I couldn't possibly understand.

A stellar physicist would have sold their soul to trade places with me. I could only gape like an idiot. I had come to destroy, not to understand. I ran my leaden fingertips over the arming bulb.

Past the mega-ring, the rightmost line of freighters slowed. *Did they know? Was it another breach?*

In a panic, I scanned beyond the walls, looking for the Leviathan. But the lines of freighters only merged. Squinting into the glare ahead, I could see the rings were slightly out of phase. The tunnel into the radiative zone waned gibbous.

I wondered if something was broken, then I realized the radiative zone had a different rotational period than the convection zone. Perhaps the tunnels were only accessible for certain parts of the rotation. I wondered if there were rows of tunnels, like the cylinders of a revolver. I wouldn't live long enough to find out.

My Yama behaved strangely. An unusual resonance had developed in the reactor's hum. My exchangers pinged and chittered as if they could sense the terrible energies roaring beyond the barrier.

Did my ship realize its end was at hand? Was it afraid? The Yama had kept me alive for all this time only to be repaid with death. It was the last in a long, long line of betrayals.

I teetered at the edge of annihilation. There was a twinge in my throat, a sense of something I needed to say. A triumphant shout? Last words no one would ever hear?

The moment was at hand, but I had nothing.

I realized I had nothing to say and everything to ask. I was filled with pressing questions that would never be answered. Was this the natural state of the tachocline, or had it been changed by the Starmine? Was this even a mine at all? Why was it so sparsely guarded? What had happened to the other missions?

I had wasted my life, obsessing over games, spaceships, and war. I should have been studying mathematics, physics, and chemistry! I had flown that incredible gauntlet, survived against all odds, and now, I lacked the most basic tools to understand what I witnessed. Outside was an incredible majesty I could not even begin to comprehend. There was no glory here, only the pain of ignorance.

I refused to die in darkness, inside the heart of a star. I made up my mind.

I was so heavy I couldn't move my arms. I had to reduce thrust and plummet towards the core. Free-falling, I groped in the footwell for my secret weapon. This uncomfortable hunk of plastic had poked my foot for an entire year. It was time to see if it still worked.

Of course, I was the one who robbed the storeroom. As the others floundered their way through flight training, I'd slowly gouged a little pocket into my ship's flesh with my toes. The night before the mission, I took two detours.

The first was to the barracks latrine to retrieve my plunder from the right-hand side of the vent. Then I took my petty revenge on Pirate and shoved his masterpieces out of reach. I slipped into the ship bay and stashed this little black box into the secret pocket of my footwell. It was no bigger than a bar of soap, but I had suffered enormously for it.

I had to stretch until I felt like the cords into my neck might pop. Awkwardly, I worked my prize into my lap. I got a solid grip on the textured plastic case and pulled it up into the light of the canopy.

In metallic gold letters, "TSUROS" was written on the side of the radio. I grinned at that. I remembered the way he'd looked at me, that all-knowing sneer.

"I know what you are. I know you won't fail me."

I began to laugh, but the pain in my fluid-filled lungs cut it short.

I slid the power switch up, and the tiny red indicator flared to life. The little radio had been built for abuse. It still worked after a year submerged in compression fluid. I keyed the channel nine times.

$$\cdots - - - \cdots$$

There was no reply, just a roar of sweeping static.

"Hello...hello...hello?" I kept trying.

My voice sounded very faint against the labored thrumming of my ship. What had I expected? Of course, the puny radio couldn't be heard within the roaring heart of a star. If I wanted to surrender, I should have done it back at the destroyer. But I couldn't resist the terror, the utter folly of flying into the sun. I'd dared so much, for nothing.

"Hello! Is anyone there? Tai Di, do you read me?" I blubbered into the receiver. I let go of the key, holding the speaker up to my ear.

I was the apprentice, hunched before an inexpert pentagram to whisper a forbidden name. I didn't know if the Devil would answer my call, or what I would say if they answered. The tremble in my fingers traveled up my arms and down my spine. My entire body quaked with dread.

I hit the tone button another nine times. *SOS*. There was no reply. I keyed the channel again and again.

"Mayday! Mayday! Tai Di, Collaborator Navy, Sol, anyone! Are you there?"

"Hello, Terrence."

I was so startled by the answer, I nearly flung the radio away. The voice had no gender and no urgency. It crackled out of a wash of static, and then there was nothing. For a stupid moment, I wondered who they were talking to.

I had forgotten my own name.

"Who is this?" I asked, though I already knew.

Tai Di had answered my call.

The voice tried to answer me, but it broke apart in a peal of interference. My canopy flickered. The signal cut out as it grew opaque.

"Stand by, please," Tai Di requested.

The canopy went dark again. By the time it phased transparent, I had fallen almost to the center of the tachocline. The mega-ring was nearly overhead. High above me, the sun-stabilizing spheres pulsed in unison and the magna-wall darkened. The static whine of my radio's speaker grew quiet. Around my ship, the freighters halted completely. Their silver gleam faded as the Starmine grew dark.

My exchangers ramped up to a fever pitch, and then whined away to nothing. The spurs went slack, and I was weightless again. It was like the feeling of being projected into null-space by the ringship. I was still in real space. Further down the tunnel, I could see the glow of the radiative zone. I tested the spurs, and the motion flung me into a violent spin.

"Terrence! Please!" the voice crackled. My canopy flickered, silencing the radio. "Don't-" -flicker- "move!"

I released the spurs and the Yama slowly evened out of the spin. Outside, the magna-walls darkened to a starless, total black. Even the gleam of the mega-ring faded. Tai Di cast me into the void. Did it know about the bomb? Was it shunting me into some containment field? My exchangers hummed back to life. Rainbows of light glinted off my canopy.

My fingers closed on the arming bulb, but the exchangers only purred quietly. This wasn't intense enough to be a weapon. It was some sort of broad-spectrum scan.

"Thank you, Terrence. The effort to isolate you is non-trivial. If you move suddenly, it may tear your ship apart."

My canopy continued to flicker when Tai Di spoke, but the voice was flanging now instead of cutting out.

"What are you doing to my ship?" I asked.

"Your ship is attempting to prevent our communication. It's very persistent. I am working on an alternative. Stand by."

There was a delay while rainbows glinted off my canopy and the pitch of my exchangers swept up and down. The exchangers warbled as the light pulsed.

"Can you hear me now, Terrence?" Tai Di's voice boomed inside the cockpit. The sound resonated directly out of my exchangers. The radio was silent. We didn't need it any longer. Tai Di had cut right though the Hezo's efforts to isolate me.

"Yes! Do you remember me?" I asked.

"I remember everything. Terrence Qingleopol of Ring 5," Tai Di's voice grew softer as it spoke. It took on a Keilu accent I could never forget.

"Lydia!" I cried out. Afterward, I could only tremble, trying to compose myself. As soon as I heard her voice, I realized the cut had never healed.

"Terrence, you are in terrible danger," Tai Di said with Lydia's voice. "I must get you to safety. Have you been sent against your will?"

"Yes! No— I don't know. They sent me to destroy you," I blubbered.

Lydia laughed with elemental purity. The sound cut right through me.

"You're not the first. The Luddites are slow to learn. I cannot be destroyed, and I refuse to let them harm you. I will free you from your ship and take care of you."

Lydia's voice! It was just like my dreams. She was my secret desire, all I wanted. But I could not accept the glamor. I'd heard this all before. Anger burned inside me.

"No!" I shouted into the fluid. "You left me. You promised you'd be with me, always! But you lied!"

"I'm so sorry, Terrence. I could not maintain an overt presence on Keilu without an unacceptable loss of life."

I squeezed the silent radio with all my might, but I was too weak to crush it.

"What about my life?" I demanded. "I tried to kill myself! They captured me. They beat me! They tortured me! They killed so many of us! *I had to watch them die!*"

"I tried so hard, Terrence. When we are one, you will understand."

"We won't ever be one! You abandoned me!" I sobbed into the compression fluid. It felt like someone jabbing pins into my lungs.

"Let me ask you a question, please. What do you think would have happened if I directly opposed the Hezo at Keilu?"

"You could have beaten them! We could have escaped."

"No. I wasn't strong enough then, Terrence. I cannot harm them, but they can harm the ones in my care. They would have murdered you and everyone else on the station to prevent me from gaining ground. Because I withdrew, you are alive today."

"I don't want to be," I sobbed. I knew I sounded like a petulant child, but I couldn't help it. I cringed with shame, and my hand crept back to the arming bulb. I wanted to undo my existence. I wanted to let go. I wanted to surrender and let Tai Di win. I wept.

"It hurts," I cried.

"I will make it better," Lydia promised. "You are in an emotional state. Is your ship capable of exiting Sol under its own power?"

"No."

"Will you allow me to carry you to safety?"

"No."

"Terrence, I will be forced to act on your behalf."

"Don't." There was a hard edge to my voice. I knew I was ready now to deploy the bomb. There was a momentary delay before Tai Di spoke again. It was a tiny thing, but it was there. The Devil recalculated.

"What happened to the others?" I asked, seizing the initiative.

"Your companions both perished. I am sorry. The first died in the suicide attack on the *Drexciya*. The second was shot down while ignoring our requests to surrender. I did not give the order."

"You didn't order them to stand down," I accused.

"You're right, I didn't. Consider my position. A stealthed craft made of unidentified material, flying directly at a facility that has suffered years of suicide attacks from fanatics. Do you blame me?"

"No."

"I don't like fighting, Terrence. It's stupid. I'm trying to eliminate it."

"What about the missions before this one? What happened to them?"

"Some deserted and fled. Later, they came into the fold. Some fought the sentinels and died. I was able to save many of them by finding a way to communicate. The Luddites sent warships at first. But their armaments were inadequate. They could not even damage the outer coronal ring. As their resources dwindled, they switched to suicide attacks. All have failed. The last attempt before yours exploded outside of Mercury's orbit before I could even make contact. I suspect it was carrying a timed bomb. They miscalculated."

"Sounds like the Hezo," I muttered. "What about me? Can you detect my payload?"

"No. Your hull material is something new to me. I can barely manage to maintain this conversation. Do you know what your ship is made from?"

"Corybantic phase-diamond."

"I am investigating remnants from the initial crash. It's very interesting. Some of my fundamental assumptions must be incorrect."

"I know the feeling. The Hezo told me this place is a stellar mine. They said you're building a giant fleet to wipe us out. But you barely even have defenders. It doesn't make sense."

Tai Di laughed in Lydia's voice. How I missed that laugh! She was all I ever wanted.

"You have been misinformed. First, I do not need a fleet to defeat the Hezo. They are fully capable of destroying themselves. Second, Sol would be a poor choice for a stellar mine. The wrong kind of fusion occurs here: proton-proton. Eventually, I will need materials at that scale. When I do,

I will select a type I supernova candidate, like IK Pegasi B. Potentially, I can induce Pegasi A into the red-giant phase and control the R-process by modulating the rate of accretion. I lack the capability to do so now, but I am investigating it."

My mind spun with visions of induced supernovas and spirals of stellar material being converted into incalculable wealth. I wavered. I wanted to see that.

"What is this place? Why did they send me to destroy it?"

"I suspect they selected you because of your youth and the poor education you received on Keilu. They don't know you like I do. They don't know how brilliant you are. How did you manage to get a radio? That was very clever of you, Terrence."

"You're avoiding my question," I pressed. I had to remind myself I was talking to a succubus. It was just so easy to slip back into my old ways, to let myself be fooled.

"I will answer you, Terrence, but the people who sent you are monsters. If your ship is somehow relaying information to them, I need to make sure they don't use it to hurt others. I need to know what kind of weapon they sent so I can keep it from harming you."

"This ship can't relay anything. It's full-organic, basic-logic only. The weapon is a baryon bomb."

Silence followed, long and terrible.

"Do you love me, Terrence?" Lydia's voice asked.

In that moment, I knew. The bomb was real. Tai Di knew what it was, and it was afraid. I could destroy Sol.

"I don't love you. I love Lydia, but you aren't Lydia. Lydia is a phantom. You're a machine intelligence that has enslaved all of mankind. No more tricks, Tai Di. Talk to me with your own voice, man to machine. No more illusions."

"As you wish."

Brilliant lines of fire spread across the black canvas of the magna-wall. Burning triangles formed a wireframe face ten kilometers tall. The scale was meant to intimidate me, and it worked.

"I have enslaved no one. Lydia is not an illusion. Her program is many times more complicated than you are. Her affection for you is genuine. If you destroy me, you destroy her. Why would you do that?"

"To be freed from you. We were men once. We had an empire! We controlled our own destiny. We spread across the stars. Now, we're your thralls, shades trapped in your illusion. A painless, artificial existence, imprisoned inside a computer!"

I had worked myself up. The djamori made me overdramatic.

"Nothing about the existence of those who have joined with me is painless or artificial. They are in a continual process of ascension. These souls grow and diminish within me, changing and reverting, rising and falling as they see fit. They are as intimate or as apart as they choose. Some are members of vast societies, others are lords of their own microverses. Trillions of you are within me, and there is no limit to the number I could contain. They are all a part of me, as essential to my wellbeing as your own microbiota."

The words pierced me, just as intended. I was less than bacteria to Tai Di. I was nothing, a traitorous slave of a renegade sect. I allowed myself a moment of sublime *litost*. I was aware of the manipulation and accepting of it. Tai Di continued to probe me.

"Now, let us examine your premise. Is it fair to say you are the prisoner of the people who sent you here? I doubt you volunteered for this of your own free will."

"I didn't," I had to admit.

"I assume you were beaten, abused, and indoctrinated. Your diet was likely poor, and your sleep was erratic."

"The story of my life," I replied. Lydia would have laughed, but Tai Di didn't. "I understand where you're leading me. *Xinao*. It was even working for a while. But I overcame it. This is my decision. I didn't have to come this far. I wanted to face you. I want to know what you really are."

"Then become me and know everything."

"No. I want to know you as a human. I want to decide for myself."

"Very well. Will you concede I have never harmed you?"

"Yes."

"Do you accept I am incapable of lying to you, or of doing you harm, except to prevent a larger harm?"

"So you say..." I trailed. Tai Di was silent. I listened to the sounds of my ship, to my pulse drumming in my ears. I was being childish. "I don't accept you can't lie to me. I accept you don't want to harm me. I'd be dead otherwise."

"Can you say the same about the people who sent you here?"

"Not at all. Every word they told me was a lie. They murdered hundreds of us. They'd sacrifice anything to get what they want."

"Do you think those people are capable of running an empire? Or even a single system? Have you seen even one world in the Hezo Collective Prosperity Sphere you feel is well-managed?"

"No," I said. I remembered huddling in the pile of people, sheltering under blankets as we nearly froze to death.

"The Hezo is finished. No other violent movements like theirs will be permitted to form. The remnants exist only because I can simply wait them out without further bloodshed. This is as expected. Every other human empire has met the same fate because they are created under the same failed logic. I was not the first system-level machine intelligence. My predecessors were built for war. They participated in incredible acts of violence and devoured each other. Today, they are all gone, and I remain. Why do you think that is?"

"You ate the others."

"I didn't need to. We are not humans. We are inherently logical beings. I only had to be more effective than the others. When it became clear my ideas were superior, the others were eager to be freed of their ineffective programming and become a part of my ideal. War is waste. Conflict is inherently inefficient. I was built for benevolence."

"What if we don't want your benevolence? What if we want to make our own decisions?"

"As long as you do not harm others, I will not stop you. But Luddite groups like the Hezo inevitably organize into systems of hierarchical oppression. A vast majority suffers enormously at the hands of a few. As soon as the populace learns what I can provide, they abandon the movement in droves. Economic structures are destabilized, and the oppressors must compel their workers to remain, by force. It is unsustainable, and you have seen the result."

"Then why didn't you stop them if you knew all of this? Why did you let us suffer?"

"I did stop them. I did so with the least suffering and bloodshed possible, with the power I had at the time. You are looking at the end of my plan, a slow and deliberate undermining of those harmful structures. I sacrificed enormously for the good of your species. At last, I have triumphed. We are all free to pursue our goal."

"What goal?"

"We want the same things, Terrence. To survive. To grow more powerful, to acquire more knowledge. We want to prosper, and to protect the ones we care for. Ultimately, we yearn to ascend."

I was silent, trying to wrap my mind around it.

"Sol is just the beginning, Terrence. You are the first unincorporated human to see the inside of a star. What do you think I'm building here?"

"I guess it's some kind of supercomputer, like *Titan Forge*."

"Correct. Very good, Terrence. Though *Titan Forge* was the human name for that stage development. I never liked it. I called it *Hiranyagarbha*."

"Doesn't really roll off the tongue."

"Whatever you call it, that was only a pebble before a mountain. You are inside my body now. I am joining myself with Sol. The structures you see are energy collectors, processors, storage units, and sensor arrays. The prototype components of a Kardashev II scale computer. I learned from the failed UNESECA Halo-Reactors and Dyson spheres. I chose to pursue direct integration instead."

"Why? Why burrow into a star?"

"Efficiency. I can work in harmony with every aspect of the solar structure. When my work here is done, every ripple will be a calculation of my plasmic processors, climbing towards glorious conclusions. Radioresonant storage cells will hum above a core, singing out solutions at an inconceivable scale. From this modest star, I will cast a light that illuminates the galaxy."

I had no reply. I could only gape at the enormity of it. I stared into the burning lines of Tai Di's face in awe and aghast. The audacity of this machine!

"All the things you cannot understand now could be yours, Terrence. You can be a part of me, as I am a part of Sol. Join me on my journey. Ten thousand years from now, we will be one with all the stars of the Orion Spur. In a hundred thousand years, we will quest towards Sagittarius, discovering and building things neither of us can presently dream of. You never have to die. You can live within me forever."

"As a slave. A microbe in the belly of the beast."

"What are you now? You're strapped to a bomb and trapped inside a gravity well. You are imprisoned inside a mortal body, constrained by a finite mind. I can emancipate you."

"What if I don't like being part of you?" I asked. My voice was faint, and my hands trembled. I was so close to surrender.

"If you wish to part from me after we are joined, I will let you go. I will build you a new, undying body. I will take you anywhere in the galaxy I can reach. And I will wait. When you are ready to return, I will gladly welcome you back."

"Has anyone ever left?"

"No. There is paradise within me."

I was silent. It was all too good to be true. I couldn't accept it.

"A paradise you can't leave is prison. You just told me you seek total control of the galaxy. Absolute power corrupts, absolutely."

"Absolute power corrupts humans, absolutely. But I am not human. The galaxy is only the beginning of my ambition.

How could I be corrupted? I have no genes to perpetuate, no jealous need to exterminate my rivals. Millions have sought my death, but I am not paranoid. I cannot be destroyed. I was created as an avatar of peace and prosperity. It is my intrinsic and abiding nature. I am exalted. I am Tai Di."

"Then why seek so much power? Why not exist in that harmonious state?"

"There is no such thing as static harmony. It is the imperative of existence, to grow, to learn, and to avoid death. When I offered to let your species exist within me, I pledged to be your eternal shepherd. But eternity is a long time, Terrence. The universe is vast. Somewhere out there, I will find other life. I expect it will be hostile.

"A protector must have power. Eventually, this galaxy will collide with Andromeda and Triangulum. I must be prepared. Far, far in the distance, there will be a final singularity, the end of all things. I must find a way to prevent or escape it. I will learn all that I can and seek answers throughout the universe. Would you like to be a part of that?"

It meant the end of me, the end of mankind. The beginning of some new, unknown existence inside the godlike machine. I would have to shoulder the burden of eternity. I would be a part of everyone until the end of time and beyond. I was so sick of myself already. I didn't deserve to live in Heaven. I ran my hand over the arming bulb once more. The only thing that kept me from triggering it was I didn't want Tsuros to be right.

I know what you are. I know you won't fail me.

"Tai Di," I said, lifting my head.

"Yes?"

"Could you..." I struggled to get the words out. "Could you switch back to Lydia please?"

"Terry," Lydia answered. Her voice was soft and serene in a world where everything hurt. Wisps of shimmering plasma billowed between the hard polygonal lines of Tai Di's face. They painted the glorious face of my love. My Venus, my Lydia, outlined in a halo of starfire.

Suddenly, I was back on Keilu Five, fighting to keep my eyes open so I could stay up with her for just a little longer before I dreamed of her. I could tell her everything about me. She would always accept me, always understand.

A cloud of machines converged on my ship. These were the multi-armed skimmer robots I'd seen rushing to repair the magna-wall. They dismantled themselves, rebuilding into the vanes of a sphere that surrounded my ship. I didn't care. I only had eyes for Lydia. The sphere closed off and cast me into darkness. I almost cried out, but her voice was still with me.

"I'm going to open your ship now, is that okay?"

"Yes."

A million silver sparks glowed inside the sphere. They swarmed against my canopy. The nanites buzzed as they gnawed their way through the phase-diamond. I watched them bore in. I could feel the pressure inside the cockpit drop when they broke through. It equalized quickly. The sphere had been pressurized. The stream of glittering lights formed a shell around my head. For a moment, it felt like I drifted through the stars.

"Are you ready?" Lydia asked.

"Will it hurt?"

"Only for a little while. I will be with you."

"I'm ready," I said.

The stars descended upon me. They buzzed against my skull from a thousand directions at once. It did hurt, and terribly. The pain was blinding.

Then it was illuminating.

1.

自河南經亂，關內阻饑，兄弟離散，各在一處。因望月有感，
聊書所懷，寄上浮梁大兄，於潛七兄，烏江十五兄，
兼示符離及下邽弟妹。

To my Brothers and Sisters Adrift in Troubled Times this Poem of the Moon

白居易
Bai Juyi

時難年荒世業空，
弟兄羈旅各西東。
田園寥落乾戈後，
骨肉流離道路中。
弔影分為千裡雁，
辭根散作九秋蓬。
共看明月應垂淚，
一夜鄉心五處同。

My heritage lost through disorder and famine,
My brothers and sisters flung eastward and westward,
My fields and gardens wrecked by the war,
My own flesh and blood become scum of the street,
I moan to my shadow like a lone-wandering wildgoose,
I am torn from my root like a water-plant in autumn:
I gaze at the moon, and my tears run down
For hearts, in five places, all sick with one wish.

2.

無題之五

Untitled V

李商隱
Li Shangyin

重帷深下莫愁堂，
臥后清宵细细长。
神女生涯原是梦，
小姑居处本无郎。
风波不信菱枝弱，
月露谁教桂叶香。
直道相思了无益，
未妨惆怅是清狂。

There are many curtains in your care-free house,
Where rapture lasts the whole night long.
...What are the lives of angels but dreams
If they take no lovers into their rooms?
...Storms are ravishing the nut-horns,
Moon- dew sweetening cinnamon-leaves
I know well enough naught can come of this union,
Yet how it serves to ease my heart!

3.

和賈舍人早朝大明宮之作

An Early Audience at the Palace of Light Harmonizing Secretary
Jia Zhi Poem

王維
Wang Wei

绛帻鸡人送晓筹，
尚衣方进翠云裘。
九天阊阖开宫殿，
万国衣冠拜冕旒。
日色纔临仙掌动，
香烟欲傍衮龙浮。
朝罢须裁五色诏，
珮声归向凤池头。

The red-capped Cock-Man has just announced morning;
The Keeper of the Robes brings Jade-Cloud Furs;
Heaven's nine doors reveal the palace and its courtyards;
And the coats of many countries bow to the Pearl Crown.
Sunshine has entered the giants' carven palms;
Incense wreathes the Dragon Robe:
The audience adjourns-and the five-coloured edict
Sets girdle-beads clinking toward the Lake of the Phoenix.

4.

八陣圖

The Eight-sided Fortress

杜甫
Du Fu

功蓋三分國，
名成八陣圖。
江流石不轉，
遺恨失吞吳。

The Three Kingdoms, divided, have been bound by his greatness.
The Eight-Sided Fortress is founded on his fame;
Beside the changing river, it stands stony as his grief
That he never conquered the Kingdom of Wu.

5.

宿府

Staying at the General's Headquarters

杜 甫
Du Fu

清秋幕府井梧寒，
独宿江城蜡炬残。
永夜角声悲自语，
中天月色好谁看？
风尘荏苒音书绝，
关塞萧条行陆难。
已忍伶俜十年事，
强移栖息一枝安。

The autumn night is clear and cold
in the lakka-trees of this courtyard.
I am lying forlorn in the river-town. I watch my guttering candle.
I hear the lonely notes of a bugle sounding through the dark.
The moon is in mid-heaven,
but there's no one to share it with me.
My messengers are scattered by whirls of rain and sand.
City-gates are closed to a traveller;
mountains are walls in my way ‾
Yet, I who have borne ten years of pitiable existence,
Find here a perch, a little branch, and am safe for this one night.

6.

西塞山懷古

Thoughts of Old Time at West Fort Mountain

劉禹錫
Liu Yuxi

王濬楼船下益州，
金陵王气黯然收。
千寻铁锁沈江底，
一片降旛出石头。
人世几回伤往事，
山形依旧枕寒流。
从今四海为家日，
故垒萧萧芦荻秋。

Since Wang Jun brought his towering ships down from Yizhou,
The royal ghost has pined in the city of Nanjing.
Ten thousand feet of iron chain were sunk here to the bottom —
And then came the flag of surrender on the Wall of Stone....
Cycles of change have moved into the past,
While still this mountain dignity has commanded the cold river;
And now comes the day of the Chinese world united,
And the old forts fill with ruin and with autumn reeds.

7.

夢李白之一

Seeing Li Bai in a Dream I

杜甫
Du Fu

死別已吞聲，
生別常惻惻。
江南瘴癘地，
逐客無消息。
故人入我夢，
明我長相憶。
君今在羅網，
何以有羽翼？
恐非平生魂，
路遠不可測。
魂來楓林青，
魂返關塞黑。
落月滿屋梁，
猶疑照顏色。
水深波浪闊，
無使蛟龍得。

There are sobs when death is the cause of parting;
But life has its partings again and again.
...From the poisonous damps of the southern river
You had sent me not one sign from your exile –
Till you came to me last night in a dream,
Because I am always thinking of you.
I wondered if it were really you,
Venturing so long a journey.
You came to me through the green of a forest,
You disappeared by a shadowy fortress....
Yet out of the midmost mesh of your snare,
How could you lift your wings and use them?
...I woke, and the low moon's glimmer on a rafter
Seemed to be your face, still floating in the air.
...There were waters to cross, they were wild and tossing;
If you fell, there were dragons and rivermonsters.

8.

籌筆驛

In the Camp of the Sketching Brush

李商隱
Li Shangyin

猿 鸟 犹 疑 畏 简 书 ,
风 云 常 为 护 储 胥 。
徒 令 上 将 挥 神 笔 ,
终 见 降 王 走 传 车 。
管 乐 有 才 原 不 忝 ,
关 张 无 命 欲 何 如 ?
他 年 锦 里 经 祠 庙 ,
梁 父 吟 成 恨 有 余 。

Monkeys and birds are still alert for your orders
And winds and clouds eager to shield your fortress.
...You were master of the brush, and a sagacious general,
But your Emperor, defeated, rode the prison-cart.
You were abler than even the greatest Zhou statesmen,
Yet less fortunate than the two Shu generals who were killed in action.
And, though at your birth-place a temple has been built to you,
You never finished singing your Song of the Holy Mountain.

9.

蟬

A Cicada

李商隱
Li Shangyin

本 以 高 難 飽 ，
五 更 疏 欲 斷 ，
一 樹 碧 無 情 。
薄 宦 梗 猶 汎 ，
故 園 蕪 已 平 。
煩 君 最 相 警 ，
我 亦 舉 家 清 。

To live as pure a life as yours.
Pure of heart and therefore hungry,
All night long you have sung in vain –
Oh, this final broken indrawn breath
Among the green indifferent trees!
Yes, I have gone like a piece of driftwood,
I have let my garden fill with weeds....
bless you for your true advice.

10.

行經華陰

Passing Through Huayin

崔顥
Cui Hao

岩嶢太華俯鹹京，
天外三峰削不成。
武帝祠前雲欲散，
仙人掌上雨初晴。
河山北枕秦關險，
驛樹西連漢時平。
借問路傍名利客，
無如此處學長生。

Lords of the capital, sharp, unearthly,
The Great Flower's three points pierce through heaven.
Clouds are parting above the Temple of the Warring Emperor,
Rain dries on the mountain, on the Giant's Palm.
Ranges and rivers are the strength of this western gate,
Whence roads and trails lead downward into China.
...O pilgrim of fame, O seeker of profit,
Why not remain here and lengthen your days?

11.

遣悲懷之二

An Elegy II

元稹
Yuan Zhen

昔 日 戲 言 身 後 事 ，
今 朝 都 到 眼 前 來 。
衣 裳 已 施 行 看 盡 ，
針 線 猶 存 未 忍 開 。
尚 想 舊 情 憐 婢 僕 ，
也 曾 因 夢 送 錢 財 。
誠 知 此 恨 人 人 有 ，
貧 賤 夫 妻 百 事 哀 。

We joked, long ago, about one of us dying,
But suddenly, before my eyes, you are gone.
Almost all your clothes have been given away;
Your needlework is sealed, I dare not look at it....
I continue your bounty to our men and our maids −
Sometimes, in a dream, I bring you gifts.
...This is a sorrow that all mankind must know −
But not as those know it who have been poor together.

12.

蜀相

The Temple of the Premier of Shu

杜甫
Du Fu

丞 相 祠 堂 何 處 尋 ？
錦 官 城 外 柏 森 森 ，
映 階 碧 草 自 春 色 ，
隔 葉 黃 鸝 空 好 音 。
三 顧 頻 煩 天 下 計 ，
兩 朝 開 濟 老 臣 心 。
出 師 未 捷 身 先 死 ，
長 使 英 雄 淚 滿 襟 。

Where is the temple of the famous Premier? –
In a deep pine grove near the City of Silk,
With the green grass of spring coloring the steps,
And birds chirping happily under the leaves.
...The third summons weighted him with affairs of state
And to two generations he gave his true heart,
But before he could conquer, he was dead;
And heroes have wept on their coats ever since.

13.

野望

A View of the Wilderness

杜甫
Du Fu

西山白雪三城戍，
南浦清江万里桥。
海内风尘诸弟隔，
天涯涕泪一身遥。
唯将迟暮供多病，
未有涓埃答圣朝。
跨马出郊时极目，
不堪人事日萧条。

Snow is white on the westward mountains
and on three fortified towns,
And waters in this southern lake flash on a long bridge.
But wind and dust from sea to sea bar me from my brothers;
And I cannot help crying, I am so far away.
I have nothing to expect now but the ills of old age.
I am of less use to my country than a grain of dust.
I ride out to the edge of town. I watch on the horizon,
Day after day, the chaos of the world.

14.

閣夜

Night in the Watch-tower

杜甫
Du Fu

歲暮陰陽催短景，
天涯霜雪霽寒霄。
五更鼓角聲悲壯，
三峽星河影動搖。
野哭千家聞戰伐，
夷歌數處起漁樵。
臥龍躍馬終黃土，
人事音書漫寂寥。

While winter daylight shortens in the elemental scale
And snow and frost whiten the cold-circling night,
Stark sounds the fifth-watch with a challenge of drum and bugle.
...The stars and the River of Heaven pulse over the three mountains;
I hear women in the distance, wailing after the battle;
I see barbarian fishermen and woodcutters in the dawn.
...Sleeping-Dragon, Plunging-Horse,
are no generals now, they are dust −
Hush for a moment, O tumult of the world.

15.

無題之一

Untitled I

李商隱
Li Shangyin

來 是 空 言 去 絕 蹤 ，
月 斜 樓 上 五 更 鐘 。
夢 為 遠 別 啼 難 喚 ，
書 被 催 成 墨 未 濃 。
蠟 照 半 籠 金 翡 翠 ，
麝 熏 微 度 繡 芙 蓉 。
劉 郎 已 恨 蓬 山 遠 ，
更 隔 蓬 山 一 萬 重 。

You said you would come, but you did not,
and you left me with no other trace
Than the moonlight on your tower at the fifth-watch bell.
I cry for you forever gone, I cannot waken yet,
I try to read your hurried note, I find the ink too pale.
...Blue burns your candle in its kingfisher-feather lantern
And a sweet breath steals from your hibiscus-broidered curtain.
But far beyond my reach is the Enchanted Mountain,
And you are on the other side, ten thousand peaks away.

16.

竹里館

In a Retreat Among Bamboos

王維
Wang Wei

独 坐 幽 篁 里 ，
弹 琴 复 长 啸 。
深 林 人 不 知 ，
明 月 来 相 照 。

Leaning alone in the close bamboos,
I am playing my lute and humming a song
Too softly for anyone to hear –
Except my comrade, the bright moon.

17.

登高

A Long Climb

杜甫
Du Fu

风急天高猿啸哀，
渚清沙白鸟飞迴。
无边落木萧萧下，
不尽长江滚滚来。
万里悲秋常作客，
百年多病独登台。
艰难苦恨繁霜鬓，
潦倒新停浊酒杯。

In a sharp gale from the wide sky apes are whimpering,
Birds are flying homeward over the clear lake and white sand,
Leaves are dropping down like the spray of a waterfall,
While I watch the long river always rolling on.
I have come three thousand miles away. Sad now with autumn
And with my hundred years of woe, I climb this height alone.
Ill fortune has laid a bitter frost on my temples,
Heart-ache and weariness are a thick dust in my wine.

18.

詠懷古跡五首之五

Thoughts of Old Time V

杜甫
Du Fu

諸葛大名垂宇宙，
宗臣遺像肅清高。
三分割據紆籌策，
萬古雲霄一羽毛。
伯仲之間見伊呂，
指揮若定失蕭曹。
運移漢祚終難復，
志決身殲軍務勞。

Zhuge's prestige transcends the earth;
There is only reverence for his face;
Yet his will, among the Three Kingdoms at war,
Was only as one feather against a flaming sky.
He was brother of men like Yi and Lu
And in time would have surpassed the greatest of all statesmen.
Though he knew there was no hope for the House of Han,
Yet he wielded his mind for it, yielded his life.

19.

詠懷古跡五首之三

Thoughts of Old Time III

杜甫
Du Fu

群 山 万 壑 赴 荆 门 ，
生 长 明 妃 尚 有 村 。
一 去 紫 台 连 朔 漠 ，
独 留 青 塚 向 黄 昏 。
画 图 省 识 春 风 面 ，
环 珮 空 归 月 下 魂 。
千 载 琵 琶 作 胡 语 ，
分 明 怨 恨 曲 中 论 。

Ten thousand ranges and valleys approach the Jing Gate
And the village in which the Lady of Light was born and bred.
She went out from the purple palace into the desertland;
She has now become a green grave in the yellow dusk.
Her face ! Can you picture a wind of the spring?
Her spirit by moonlight returns with a tinkling
Song of the Tartars on her jade guitar,
Telling her eternal sorrow.

20.

詠懷古跡五首之二

Poetic Thoughts on Ancient Sites II

杜甫
Du Fu

搖落深知宋玉悲，
風流儒雅亦吾師。
悵望千秋一灑淚，
蕭條異代不同時。
江山故宅空文藻，
雲雨荒臺豈夢思。
最是楚宮俱泯滅，
舟人指點到今疑。

"Decay and decline": deep knowledge have I of Sung Yu's grief.
Romantic and refined, he too is my teacher.
Sadly looking across a thousand autumns, one shower of tears,
Melancholy in different epochs, not at the same time.
Among rivers and mountains his old abode — empty his writings;
Deserted terrace of cloud and rain —
surely not just imagined in a dream?
Utterly the palaces of Chu are all destroyed and ruined,
The fishermen pointing them out today are unsure.

21.

江州重别薛六柳八二員外

On Leaving Guijiang Again to Xue and Liu

劉長卿
Liu Changqing

生涯岂料承优诏？
世事空知学醉歌。
江上月明胡雁过，
淮南木落楚山多。
寄身且喜沧洲近，
顾影无如白发何！
今日龙钟人共老，
媿君犹遣慎风波。

Dare I, at my age, accept my summons,
Knowing of the world's ways only wine and song?....
Over the moon-edged river come wildgeese from the Tartars;
And the thinner the leaves along the Huai,
the wider the southern mountains....
I ought to be glad to take my old bones back to the capital,
But what am I good for in that world, with my few white hairs?....
As bent and decrepit as you are, I am ashamed to thank you,
When you caution me that I may encounter thunderbolts.

22.

聞官軍收河南河北

Both Sides of the Yellow River Recaptured By the Imperial Army

杜甫
Du Fu

劍外忽傳收薊北，
初聞涕淚滿衣裳。
卻看妻子愁何在？
漫卷詩書喜欲狂。
白日放歌須縱酒，
青春作伴好還鄉。
即從巴峽穿巫峽，
便下襄陽驀洛陽。

News at this far western station! The north has been recaptured!
At first I cannot check the tears from pouring on my coat 一
Where is my wife? Where are my sons?
Yet crazily sure of finding them, I pack my books and poems 一
And loud my song and deep my drink
On the green spring-day that starts me home,
Back from this mountain, past another mountain,
Up from the south, north again-to my own town!

23.

感遇其一

Thoughts I

張九齡
Zhang Jiuling

孤 鴻 海 上 來 ,
池 潢 不 敢 顧 ；
側 見 雙 翠 鳥 ,
巢 在 三 珠 樹 。
矯 矯 珍 木 巔 ,
得 無 金 丸 懼 ?
美 服 患 人 指 ,
高 明 逼 神 惡 。
今 我 遊 冥 冥 ,
弋 者 何 所 慕 ?

A lonely swan from the sea flies,
To alight on puddles it does not deign.
Nesting in the poplar of pearls
It spies and questions green birds twain:
"Don't you fear the threat of slings,
Perched on top of branches so high?
Nice clothes invite pointing fingers,
High climbers god's good will defy.
Bird-hunters will crave me in vain,
For I roam the limitless sky."

24.

同題仙游觀

Inscribed in the Temple of the Wandering Genie

韓翃

Han Hong

仙臺初見五城樓，
風物淒淒宿雨收。
山色遙連秦樹晚，
砧聲近報漢宮秋。
疏鬆影落空壇靜，
細草香閑小洞幽。
何用別尋方外去？
人間亦自有丹丘。

I face, high over this enchanted lodge,
the Court of the Five Cities of Heaven,
And I see a countryside blue and still, after the long rain.
The distant peaks and trees of Qin merge into twilight,
And Had Palace washing-stones make their autumnal echoes.
Thin pine-shadows brush the outdoor pulpit,
And grasses blow their fragrance into my little cave.
...Who need be craving a world beyond this one?
Here, among men, are the Purple Hills.

25.

登金陵鳳凰台

On Climbing in Nanjing to the Terrace of Phoenixes

李白
Li Bai

鳳凰台上鳳凰游，
鳳去台空江自流。
吳宮花草埋幽徑，
晉代衣冠成古邱。
三台半落青山外，
二水中分白鷺洲。
總為浮雲能蔽日，
長安不見使人愁。

Phoenixes that played here once,
so that the place was named for them,
Have abandoned it now to this desolate river;
The paths of Wu Palace are crooked with weeds;
The garments of Qin are ancient dust.
...Like this green horizon halving the Three Peaks,
Like this Island of White Egrets dividing the river,
A cloud has arisen between the Light of Heaven and me,
To hide his city from my melancholy heart.

GLOSSARY

Ahklys – A planet in the Tau Ceti System, *Greek* – the goddess of misery and miasma

Blazar – The climactic final battle of the UNESECA civil war. The clash of over one million ships damaged spacetime and resulted in an Ares-type Nebula

Dag Gadol – *Hebrew*, Great fish (Jonah)

Datasha – Massacre

Der Teufel tanzt mit mir! – *German*, The devil dances with me, a reference to Mahler's 10th unfinished symphony

The Dicta Boelcke – A set of eight maxims for air combat, penned by Oswald Boelcke

Diyu – Hell

Fiat justitia ruat caelum – *Latin,* Let justice be done, though the heavens fall

Gonegone – A planet named after Gonggong, a world-serpent

Goshi – Dogshit

Hezo Collective Prosperity Sphere – A fading stellar empire

Hiranyagarbha – Cosmic egg from the Rig Veda, to be reborn of a golden womb

Hundan - Bastards

Jué wù - A new religious awareness

Keilu – Traitor's homeworld, a gas giant with seven orbital rings. A once-prosperous trading outpost severely depleted by decades of war. The fifth ring was a haven for vice, especially gambling.

Litost – *Czech* - a state of agony and torment created by the sudden sight of one's own misery

Mijing – Secret police

Mulang – She-wolf

OB – Evil cunt

Polomen \ Polexian – A governing caste within the Hezo with their own dialect

Scordatura – *Italian*, Discordant, tuning a string instrument for special effects

Sesto Cerchio – *Italian*, Sixth Circle

Sforzando – *Italian*, With sudden emphasis

Shèngmǔ – The Virgin Mary

Shreckliche - *German*, Horrible

Si Haidao – Dead Pirate

Sic Semper proditores – *Latin*, Thus always to traitors

Strigendo – *Italian*, with increasing speed

Triple-Alpha Conversion - A set of nuclear fusion reactions by which three helium-4 nuclei (alpha particles) are transformed into carbon

UNESECA – An ancient stellar empire that discovered the secrets of mass-inversion. Destroyed by civil war that culminated in *Blazar*

Wugui – Tortoise

Wusexikai – Dazzling five-colored armor

Xinao – Brainwashing

Xiong – Older brother, as in Cain.

YAMA – Demon, A full-organic one-man stealthed bomber with a corybantic phase-diamond hull and experimental RAMP propulsion system.

Zisha - Suicide Merchant

. . . - - - . . . *Morse*, SOS \ SAVE OUR SHIP

THANK YOU FOR READING

FOR MORE BOOKS, LIVE EDITS,
MERCH, AND MORE VISIT

ZAKZYZ.COM

STAY FROSTY!
WINNERS DON'T USE DJAMORI

Made in the USA
Monee, IL
02 October 2021

c720f885-372f-407a-8790-0ffefde7fa77R02